YEAR'S BE⌣.
AOTEAROA
NEW ZEALAND
SCIENCE FICTION
& FANTASY

YEAR'S BEST AOTEAROA NEW ZEALAND SCIENCE FICTION & FANTASY

V1 / EDITED BY MARIE HODGKINSON

PAPER
ROAD
PRESS

Year's Best Aotearoa New Zealand Science Fiction and Fantasy: Volume I
edited by Marie Hodgkinson

First published in paperback and ebook in 2019
ISBN 9780473491260

Paper Road Press
paperroadpress.co.nz

Cover art by and © Emma Weakley 2019
Cover and internal design by Marie Hodgkinson

CONTENTS

Editorial *Marie Hodgkinson*   1

We Feed the Bears of Fire and Ice *Octavia Cade*   3

Trees *Toni Wi*   18

The Garden *Isabelle McNeur*   20

Logistics *A.J. Fitzwater*   30

The Billows of Sarto *Sean Monaghan*   50

A Most Elegant Solution *M. Darusha Wehm*   74

A Brighter Future *Grant Stone*   82

The Glassblower's Peace *James Rowland*   113

Mirror Mirror *Mark English*   139

Common Denominator *Melanie Harding-Shaw*   151

The People Between the Silences *Dave Moore*   155

Te Ika *J.C. Hart*   162

Girls Who Do Not Drown *Andi C. Buchanan*   180

About the Authors   191

Acknowledgements   195

Also from Paper Road Press   197

EDITORIAL

Every year, writers from Aotearoa New Zealand have their stories snapped up by publishers across the globe. These stories make it onto honours lists and are widely recommended and critically acclaimed, and then...

Well.

Things are seldom lost forever on the internet, but they certainly become harder to find. And it is all too easy for stories that shine like shooting stars to fade like them, too.

I wanted to change that.

This book is the first volume of an annual anthology series that will bring new life and new light to the best science fiction and fantasy to come out of this country each year.

In these pages you'll find stories of apocalypse and survival, hope and bitter retribution; of people living in the spaces left behind and building new spaces to fit what they are or have become.

It's not always the world that changes; sometimes, it's us, and the change may be monstrous or welcome – or monstrously welcome.

I'll leave it up to you to decide which stories fit which description.

My heartfelt thanks go out to all the authors, editors and publishers around the world whose hard work allowed me to put together this anthology, and to Emma Weakley, whose gorgeous artwork graces its cover. More than that, thanks are due to everyone who has supported Paper Road Press over the years. The publishing landscape has changed hugely in the six years since Paper Road Press started publishing and it shows no signs of stopping. As a small press at the edge of the world, the support of readers, booksellers and libraries remains key to our success.

So, here's to you, and here's to hoping you enjoy this latest collection.

These thirteen stories are my top picks for 2018, but they're neither the be-all nor the end-all of SFF writing in this country.

They're only the beginning.

Marie Hodgkinson
Paper Road Press

WE FEED THE BEARS OF FIRE AND ICE
OCTAVIA CADE

Look at what we woke.

* * *

We feed them lies and watch them burn for it.

Koala bears rarely run during bush fires. Their instinct at danger is to climb up into canopy, where the leaves are shot through with eucalyptus oil, and flammable. They cling to the trunk with charred paws when it begins to burn, the thin bark catching easily and falling off in flaming strips. It sets their fur alight.

They die screaming.

* * *

Polar bears need pack ice to hunt. When the ice breaks up they swim until their strength runs out, or pull themselves onto continent and walk until their muscles waste, until they drag their back legs behind them and fur fails to cover their ribs. They're too slow and too starved to find food, and they drag themselves along until they can't anymore.

They die without the strength to scream.

* * *

Look at what we woke.

* * *

Darwin is now called The City of Fire. Thermal imagery photographs show red streams through the streets, along the exposed surfaces of buildings. These are as hot as 70°C, and we who still live and work in Darwin do so underground. Sewers have been hollowed further, pipes opened up into giant arching chambers beneath the steaming soil, and at each entrance are thick grates, and guarded, because the saltwater crocodiles swim underground as well, with the sewers opening up to the sea and the stormwater drains – dusty for most of the year, until hurricane season – letting the smaller ones slip through.

They grow large beneath, as the fires grow large above.

* * *

The ground is wetter. It holds the chill less, and bread baskets move north. More of the lands under long sun are opened up for agriculture, farmers moving slowly polewards, for climate has changed the patterns of growing and there are places that once produced that don't anymore, or don't so much, and Canada has water to spare now which is more than can be said for California, reenacting Steinbeck as its vineyards wither. The further north we move, out of heat and into wilderness, the more susceptible we are to being eaten rather than eating ourselves.

The more we come to think it's deserved. After all, we let it happen.

* * *

Scientific American, 8 February 2016: <u>Australia Cuts 110 Climate Scientist Jobs</u>

* * *

Sacrifices have to be made. We didn't do it then, so we have to do it now.

Our ancestors, some of them, tied their heretics to posts and placed kindling around them, lit them up as candles for punishment. Our sacrifice is not religious, but when we fasten a person to their own fire-stake and stack eucalyptus leaves around their feet, leave them wailing through the heat of day until the fire comes for them, the impulse is no different. Propitiation, atonement, mercy.

Sometimes heatstroke renders them insensible before the fire comes. Sometimes we think these are the better days, but sometimes we build our altars in the early morning, set them in places where we can see the sparks already settling, because sacrifice, we think, should be screaming.

* * *

Our ancestors, some of them, starved the criminals and the people they claimed as useless, denied them food in times of short resource, let them go out into the wild and the dark to die alone, or to survive as best they could away from community. Now when we leave a person to exposure we take no chances of them coming back. We leave them in the wilderness, strip them naked, slash the tendons in the backs of their legs so that they can only crawl away from the starving bear that their blood calls.

Most often shock and blood loss leaves them unconscious; they don't feel the claws and the jaws and the tearing. And sometimes the silence is better even, because sacrifice, we think, should not always draw attention to itself with screaming.

* * *

Lies have such a monstrous *weight*.

We knew what we were doing. We didn't know what would come of it.

Monsters are too busy lying to think ahead.

* * *

The koala comes with burning.

It stalks through the streets, its body the size of skyscrapers, and we've watched it bring those flaming feet down and braced for impact and earthquakes, because something that size should shatter the balance of small-minded things when it moves, but for all fire comes with noise and substance all the conflagration is above ground.

All we do is wrap our heads with wet cloth and crouch beneath, watch the koala as it burns itself out and takes the city with it.

* * *

Hunger comes down from the north, an enormous frozen mouth with teeth like icicles. It paces over ice with furry paws, stretches enormous over countryside. We watch as it walks overhead, the hunger bear, and its famine claws leave furrows waist deep in the earth. Its head the size of houses, it breathes starvation and we starve under it, or think we do, for the hunger bear was raised with lies and breathes the same through those sharp and unhappy teeth.

When we feel that breath like wind on our own faces we chain ourselves to fridges, not only for the potential for gorging, but because once we've eaten everything within reach it makes us want to walk north, north, and feed ourselves to what we've starved.

* * *

Look at what we woke.
Look at what we *made*.

* * *

Ghost bears, giant bears, pacing over landscape. They burn and hunt and eat, their paws and eucalyptus breath, their scars and starving claws.

We blister under them. We bleed and freeze. They take no notice. We're so small, compared to them, to the blizzards and firestorms of their bodies. No wonder they see us as nothing but fuel.

We feed them pieces of ourselves. Sacrificial offerings, to make them go away.

Sometimes it even works.

* * *

The stake, the bones and flesh and screaming, are always burned to ash. These blow away in scalding winds, the ground baked so hard that it's hard for us to dig the next hole, to set the next post. It's a filthy job and an unhappy one, but we do it because the circle of blackened earth around the post is large, but often limited. More often than not, once the red bear eats it blows itself out, doesn't drag that massive body through the rest of Darwin, doesn't burn what remains of city and fields and food stores, the fishing docks down at the harbour.

One of us burns, or we all do.

* * *

The jaws of the hunger bear bite through bone as though it is a soft and spongy thing. We hear it eat, out on the remains of ice, though the exposed, the ones with their tendons cut, are little more than mouthfuls. But sacrifice never meant satiation, which is all to the good as there's nothing that could fill up the hunger bear anyway, and if we didn't keep it away with blood-offering it would loom over all our cities, would bring its great paw down on houses and schools and shops until we all ran out, swarmed out of our little places like termites, knowing that it meant being devoured but the emptiness in our guts is a promise that devouring is the quicker option, the kinder death.

One of us feeds, or we all do. Every day we feed, because every day we lied.

* * *

Science, 25 August 2017: <u>DOE Denies It Has Policy to Remove 'Climate Change' from Agency Materials</u>
   The Scientist, 29 August 2017: <u>Researchers Advised to Remove Climate Change Language</u>

* * *

Every day we lied, and every day we used truth to do it:
   Bears have died for climate before. The giant koala, *Phascolarctos stirtoni*, is a Pleistocene relative of today's koala. Its common name is relative, for the giant koala was only a third again as large as its modern kin, not near as large as the holocaust in koala shape that stalks our cities, but size didn't save it in the end. It is hypothesised that the giant koala died because the climate changed, because of the effect that change had on sources of nutrition.
   (Today, increased atmospheric carbon dioxide reduces the nutrients available in eucalyptus leaves, increases the amount of toxic tannins. There's starvation here as well, and poison to go with burning, the dehydration deaths caused by leaves with too little water.)

* * *

Bears have lived for climate before. Late in the Pleistocene, a population of brown bears, *Ursus arctos*, adapted to the ecology of their polar home. They began to eat a diet that was primarily meat, primarily marine, and their ability to process large amounts of animal fat without cardio-pulmonary consequence developed, differentiating them from their brown cousins. Their fur lightened, their molars changed. A new species, and an iconic one, bred on the border lines of ice age.

(Today, increasing temperatures lead to loss of ice and the polar bears are moving inland, into brown bear territory. The two interbreed, producing fertile offspring and suggesting that genetic change has not yet reached true species-level difference.)

* * *

This is how it goes: Climate change is a hack, a fraud, a politically motivated recipe for economic failure. It's happened in the past, without us, for billions of years the climate changed without us. We can't affect the climate, we're only one species and the world is so large and so complex, and besides, God would never allow it.

It's bad science. It's hippie emotionalism. Species come and go, and humans are the only important one anyway. Organisms that can't adapt to changing conditions should just die. It's sad, but it's not our fault.

* * *

Photographs of koalas with burned paws are shared around the world. We watch them being given water from a fireman's drink bottle, watch them face down on a veterinary table with each paw soaking in little tubs, wearing colourful protective wee mittens over bandages and burned flesh, and donations of those home-made mittens are sent from far-off countries. Hundreds of mittens, thousands of them, and it's an easy way for us to put off responsibility, pretending that helping in small ways makes up for refusing the large ones.

(The small helps are necessary too.)

* * *

The starving bears tug heartstrings. There's a guilt that's hard to look at, so when they take someone who's wandered too close, the waves of meat moving north, we look away and try not to blame. It's easier to refuse responsibility when the refusal's on both sides, and the bears never take a lot.

There's not enough of them left to make a dent, in any case.

(Forgiveness can sometimes be stronger than fear.)

* * *

If we don't look, everything is normal. If we don't look, it's not happening.

* * *

Scientific American, 31 October 2017: <u>Government Scientist Blocked from Talking About Climate and Wildfires</u>

* * *

The ecology of Australia is adapted to fire. Its evolution is one of burning. The eucalypts, especially, are serotinous. The seeds survive bushfires in woody casings that open after flames. The leaves take a long time to break down and are impregnated with flammable oils; the bark shreds off in thin pieces. Alight, they can be blown over distance.

One lit match, and the fire will spread and spread.

(Organisms that can't adapt to changing conditions should just die.)

We have adapted to fire.

We volunteer for burning, when the crocodiles have taken our families, when the fire has taken our features. Our world is one of sunlight anyway, of pain and burning and it is the world of our creation, the world which our lies have made. When the fire koala breathes on us, hot gusts in our faces set our hair alight, set our lungs to scalding and the screaming stops then, our hands still tugging futile at the stake they've been tied to and we die in sizzling clouds of eucalyptus oil with the claws and burning fur of the koala brushing up against us.

All our extremes were *normal*, they said.

* * *

The ecology of the Arctic is adapted to ice. Its evolution is one of dry freezing: permafrost, glaciers, sea ice, the frigid oceanic currents. Bearded seals are a favourite food of polar bears. The seals are able to survive the cold primarily due to their thick layers of blubber, a highly calorific fat content that makes them valuable prey for marine carnivores. The increasing temperatures and subsequent reduction in ice means that the bearded seals are harder to stalk, and harder to catch.

Organisms that can't adapt to changing conditions should just die, they said.

We have adapted to ice loss.

We volunteer for exposure when the hunger grows too great, when our children have opened up their bellies with scalpels to pack the food in deeper, when their blood on our hands has a meaty, delicious flavour. When the hunger bear stands over us, body big enough to block out the sun and its ribs poking through the horror-structure of its body, the screams are frozen in our lungs, full of icicles now and longing. The last thing we smell is our bellies, opened up and steaming, the enticement of blood and our own fingers tearing at bowels, the nails not long enough to really join in the feasting.

Catastrophic extremes are only to be expected, they said.

* * *

The bears, the bears.

We feed the bears of fire and ice, we feed them lies, we feed them twice.

We lied and woke them up.

* * *

Heatstroke takes more lives than invasion. Underground is cooler, but we can't stay there forever and even those south of us are burning in their cities. There's transport, supplies come in from other places, the remains of growing things for food. It's easier at night when the heat gnaws less at bones but crocodiles are night hunters and they're growing larger, and there aren't enough night vision goggles to keep their silent, heavy tread away.

It's safer in sunlight, barely, but the heatstroke bites with red teeth, more dangerous than mouths.

Hunger takes more lives than invasion. For all the landscape's changing, the wild places getting smaller and crowding the animals into our back yards, making them walk our streets, it doesn't stop us eating. That's the life instinct: to go on, to consume, and some of us don't have enough and die of it, while some of us have more than enough and it's still not, because the long snout of hunger lies beneath and ready to ambush. It wakes us in the night and sets us to stuffing, makes us burst our own bellies with the lies we fed ourselves, makes us walk out into dark streets where the wolves scavenge, where the brown bears lie in wait.

It's safer in sunlight, but who wants to spend all their life with clear vision anyway. Our vision is already clear enough.

* * *

We came for them first, the ones who lied the best.

We had to. Every organism adapts to their environment; it was a matter of survival. Sacrifice means the holocaust above dies down at night. Even the buildings cool, the tar settles in the streets and come early morning we can walk across it without sticking, with the crocodile tracks and the great marks of the fire bear as it drags its claws through the city stand rigid around us before the roads melt again into straightness. The fire bear always comes back during the day. It stays away longer if we give it something new to consume … something not eucalypt because we raised the fire bear on lies and that's what it likes best to eat.

It dies down in winter, the hunger storm without, the frozen winds. The ice that's left reforms, the polar bears that are left scramble to the floes for hunting, but the summer always comes back with starvation and they have to come for us instead. And we had to come for them – for the ones who lied the best, because if we lie as slick as seals the lies seep out of us like so much oily blubber, give a shiny bursting gloss to skin. The more the hunger bear eats of lies, the longer the winters last.

This makes us careful about our lies, doling them out in small proportion when once we spewed and swallowed them like the smell of eucalyptus leaves, like the soft giving flesh of fat and fish.

* * *

The Guardian, 26 May 2016: <u>Australia Scrubbed from UN Climate Change Report after Government Intervention</u>

* * *

I'm a liar too. A koala is a marsupial, not a bear.

Tourist dollars, industry profits, narrative structure. Whatever it's for, we lie to make a point.

* * *

The ones of us who know we are liars, well. We begin to think of justice, because if ever there is an ideal constructed out of falsity it is that, and we are all familiar.

Justice becomes a temptation, and a cause.

We set fire to them first, the worst of the liars. When the city started burning down, when it was too hot to live above ground and those monstrous footprints started burning city blocks we dragged out the politicians who'd signed and bribed and looked away, strung them from lamp-posts with their guts cut out and hanging down, set fire to their entrails while they were still living because the screaming brought the bear from the suburbs, from the supermarkets, from trying to force its face through grating into the drains where we huddled, the iron glowing and bending sticky-soft around that searching face.

We took knives to them first, the polluters and the lobbyists, the ones that we let look away for profit, the ones whose money we took to look away in turn, but money didn't do much for us when the hunger bear came and it didn't do much for them either, didn't patch together their tendons with bank notes as the bear stalked them bloody, didn't let them call for help because we stuffed their gullets before we cut them, pouched their cheeks with promissory notes the colour of bribes and lies, the ones that said they could buy anything, including bears.

But bears cannot be bought. Which is why, when we look at them, we see the mirrors in their starved and burning eyes, the ones that say we let it happen, we let our greed and their greed call the bears and now they've come and we've nothing left but sacrifice.

* * *

Hot breath against cheek. *Was it worth it*, says the koala, its body the size of skyscrapers.

Cold claw against stomach. *How do your lies taste now*, says the polar bear, its head the size of houses.

* * *

They taste like ice and ashes. They taste like the breath of the bear that ate our homework. The payment's in the post the email never came it was fire-based ecology anyway we don't feel well not all scientists agree a bear ate our grandmother died after eating homework glaciers have always come and gone the car wouldn't start there's an accident on the roads danger to the economy we'll be right there with the money homework promises these extremes are normal ate our homework it would have happened anyway five minutes we'll be there in *five minutes* of course we didn't mean it like that one person can't do anything one species better you than us better them than us it'll be over soon…
This is how it goes.

* * *

Look at what we woke.
Look at what we woke *in us*.

* * *

There's a lot less liars now.

TREES
TONI WI

We bleed the trees in the evening. If we left them overnight they'd be fat, bloated carcases by the morning. Bloody trees attract predators. It's a vile job, but it has to be done.

If you're not careful you get blood all over you.

Tree blood doesn't smell like trees. It smells like dying. Like the dead rat the cat hid under the back porch last summer. Like something that was alive, until it wasn't.

We try not to think about it, considering all the trees we've cut down over the years. If the tree is alive, if it bleeds like living things do, then maybe it can think like living things do as well.

I try not to imagine where the eyes would be. What it would say, if it had a mouth. What it would do if it had teeth.

The things that eat trees are not the kinds of things we want around at night time, so we have to bleed the trees before the dark settles in. But you can't do it too early, either. The blood is in the leaves during the day. By sunset, it starts to drain back down to the roots. We siphon it off before it gets down too deep, before it clots. Before it builds. A red pressure. Deep down, beneath the earth.

Once, when I was younger, I forgot to drain the tree in our back yard. It was an ugly, half-dead old thing; a grandaddy tree.

It came with the house when we moved in. Not many places still had trees, even back then. Most home-owners had them removed. With proper maintenance though, you could still own a home *and* a tree. I was playing out back, and my Mother reminded me to drain the tree before I came in for the night. But I was a boy, and easily distracted. By the time I sat down at the dinner table I had forgotten all about it.

There was a crack in the night, like thunder, that woke me from my sleep. It was a sound of gods tearing each other limb from limb. I bolted out of bed to the window, flinging back the curtains. The moon was out, a pale blue ghost watching from above. And there, near the back fence, was the husk of the old tree. One whole side of it was gone, and the other had sagged over so the branches were touching the ground. It had split down the middle. Blood was spurting from the stump, right up in the air like a geyser. A howl cut through the night, and then another. I fell from the window and retched up my dinner.

No-one knows where the blood came from. People say it was something in the water, after all the biological fighting. The religious believe it's a curse on humanity – a sign of the end of days.

But it doesn't feel so much like an apocalypse. It feels more like a defence mechanism. Mother Earth, protecting her own.

We bleed, she says. And we know.

THE GARDEN
ISABELLE MCNEUR

Later, we tried to console ourselves with it: we went into this knowing that when we got home everyone we knew would be old or dead. We coped in different ways – some of us chose to draw away, numbing a wound before the shock wore off, where others spent their last days with them.

Adams left a wife and a kid behind. I don't know how he did it. I had enough trouble leaving my dog. For the first time in my life I had been glad my parents had already passed.

The lights were off when we stumbled out of those cryo pods. Someone started this breathless giggling as I was feeling my way around for the emergency exit. I had to stop myself from smiling along with it: nerves did that, as much as they tried to train it out of us. I remember way back on my first spacewalk, an impossible amount of nothingness on all sides, thinking about how this spacesuit was the only thing between me and dying ugly, and I burst out in gulping laughs long enough that someone came on the comms to check if I was okay.

Finally I got the door open and the five of us – back when it was still Hyung, Adams, Johnson, Garcia and me – climbed into the sun, squinting. There was no-one rushing up to apologise for the malfunction or lack of communication. There was no-one when we crossed the tarmac to the main buildings. Vines had crawled up to the roof.

We shouted, banged on the walls. Eventually one of us – I think it was Garcia, our pilot – smashed a window in. Inside was a scene that would scream normal if it wasn't for the things out of place. It was the usual stuff: a baked-dirt stench rising from the carpet. A lunchbox sat open beside a laptop, its contents long rotted. Like the security cameras, the desks and ceilings were caked with dust.

Someone said, "Maybe everyone's out for lunch." It was probably Hyung. Whoever it was, they got an elbow in the ribs.

We got to work. Everyone choked their nerves into something controllable and focused on what was right in front of us: the power was down. There was no sign anyone was receiving our comm transmissions, NASA or otherwise. When we managed to scrounge a battery radio, static blared from every station.

By then, we weren't trading those anxious grins. Everyone kept glancing towards me with something they wouldn't admit was hope, and I tried to look every inch their Commander. I sent Hyung, our missions specialist, to check for a generator; then Johnson, the scientist, to scavenge for anything close to a clue of what had happened. I sent Adams, the engineer, to see if the cars in the parking lot still worked.

They didn't. Even if they did, a quick sniff had us confirming that the gas had long since gone off.

In the end, we walked. It took less than a day before we gave in to the fact that Washington, D.C. was empty. Skyscrapers remained, as did fast food restaurants and monuments, but they were spiderweb-ridden and completely lacking in people. The webs were a comfort: insects, at least, had survived.

People and sound: something I never thought I'd see D.C. without. There were no dogs barking. No distant car alarms or fire trucks honking or cell phones going off. There were no hotdog-festooned mascots handing out posters and yelling; no activists shelling out brochures and calling for action; no grocery bags being dropped or skateboards chiming down a metal railing or music trilling from a nearby store; nothing, nothing, nothing.

As we walked, I eyed the plants and the insects. Without people, they had taken over: bees, it seemed, were no longer in danger of extinction. The air wasn't thick with flies, which meant spiders were still in traction. The usual city-faring plants burst out of buildings and slits in the sidewalks. Moss coated entire apartment blocks. A stray potato plant sat in the middle of a park. I remember holding one of its leaves between my fingers. It felt like, if not hope, then something like it.

By the time we left the city limits of D.C. the possibility of finding people had become less than hypothetical. We raided supermarkets and found sturdier shoes and piled supplies into stolen backpacks. Were they stolen if there was no-one left to steal from?

Cars lay in the middle of the road. It was the anatomy of normal rush-hour traffic, not the get-out-of-the-city brand we had been imagining.

"Rapture," Hyung suggested. She leaned inside the open window of a car and emerged with overlarge black sunglasses that made her look like a fruit fly.

Adams shook his head. "With *everyone* going up to Heaven?"

"Okay," Hyung said after a moment. "Maybe everyone who didn't qualify got sucked downwards."

We laughed, but there have been times when all of us have

considered it. Some days, it's as plausible as any other option.

Two days into our new reality we found a dead dog: a collie. Its tongue was lolling out, its eyes black with flies. It could've been alive when we landed. One of them meant there had to be more.

Dogs and plants, I remember thinking. It couldn't be too bad a world.

Out loud, I said we should keep moving. We lapsed into the usual discussions we'd have back then, the kind that have long since worn dry in favour of suggestion we upgrade the solar panels – scientific observations, suggestions, theories. Mammals still exist, not just insects, what did that add to the hypothesis that we were inventing?

Back then, no matter where I slept, I dreamed of people vanishing where they stood: pouring cereal or paying at a counter, then next minute milk is glugging over the floor and a credit card clatters against the linoleum. I still have those dreams. A few times a year I'll get that old throb, but it's been long enough now that it's more of an itch.

God. We came up with some desperate theories over the years. Some of them plausible, some of them stretching believability just so we could grab at a reason, any reason *why*. It stayed with some of us, the not knowing.

It was why Johnson left us nine years back. She was going to get a boat working and try to make physical contact with other continents rather than rely on radio towers. It's not the first time one of us has left, but it's the longest anyone has stayed gone. Most of us return before the three-year mark. None of us have found the gleaming answer to why we came home to find it deserted.

We slept in abandoned houses and cars and occasionally tents we'd set up at the side of the road. Every morning I'd wake up and do a headcount. Every morning my crew would be right where I left them, but I've never stopped checking.

We crossed state lines. We considered crossing oceans. When we reached a beach we took our shoes off and pushed our feet into the wet sand. The sea licked our heels and I tipped my head up: the sun was the same. When they came out the stars were map-worthy, still. Whatever happened down here hadn't affected things up there.

I remember sitting on that beach and thinking of Proxima Centauri B, the tiny HUB we'd left there. I told the others I missed the view from the impenetrable windows.

Hyung said, "What, you mean the never-ending darkness? I'll be honest, that scared the Jesus out of me."

"Bejeezus," Adams corrected, and she stared pointedly at him until he gave one of his rare grins and took it back.

I told her I had found it almost comforting, and Garcia agreed.

Hyung declared us both strange and pulled Adams with her to lie down in the sand. Her hair made a soft cushion under her head and she'd find sand in her hair for days afterwards. One morning she shook it out over my breakfast as punishment for eating the last of her favourite cereal.

God. I do miss that woman.

Our voyage to Proxima Centauri B had been to gather information: get hands on evidence on whether or not humanity could form a colony there.

Nowadays I like to think we aren't the only ones left, that humanity is out there exploring the stars. Maybe they'd come

24

across Proxima Centauri B one day. Would anyone find the HUB? Would humans find it if they were out there? Would they see it and remember *the Terra crew, shit, we forgot—*

It could happen someday. Maybe it already has and they're on their way. They won't get here in time. Still, I want to leave something behind for them to find, just in case.

It took a little over four months for us to tire of searching for another face. We took a group vote on whether to stay in one place for the next few weeks, and it was a non-event: we had nothing but time now. Searching could wait and we always had the radio, which Adams continued to upgrade the best he could.

We found a hospital and wired up the backup generator. I don't remember much about those weeks. There was a family of possums living in the first room I tried to sleep in. We cobbled solar panels together when the generator failed. We reminisced about our favourite sitcoms and failed to recreate *Whose Line Is it Anyway.*

What I do remember is moving the solar panels to a nearby house. Adams started to work on an easy water supply that didn't involve looting supermarkets for plastic bottles. I remember it felt solid; the hint of a future we could walk towards. I stood on the porch of that house and looked into the wild backyard. There was a cow chewing grass near one of the fences and a cluster of sunflowers overtook almost everything else.

It took days for me to find the remains of a garden bed. The planks surrounding it had been eaten through by bugs. I saw a scrap of something: an old packet that would've once declared what was growing here. It was too faded to read, but I caught a flash of waxy gold.

I touched the soil and imagined something growing up

towards my hand.

I raided the local library for books on gardening. This was back when I still felt a lingering guilt about smashing the sliding glass doors.

There was no librarian to ask and no online catalogue, so I wandered the shelves and climbed long-still escalators until I found the right section. I packed six books into a pack and sped up when I passed the dead security frames on my way out. Old habits.

On the walk home, I watched the plants that had taken over. When I was younger I'd stand in one place and imagine what it had looked like before street signs and asphalt, back when it was all animal calls and forest. What would this place look like in another thousand years?

I came to a stop in the middle of an intersection. Cars were in mid-turn: a still life painting. In another thousand years, the world would reclaim most of this. Monuments would be nests for birds before they deteriorated. Plants would dismantle the city architecture. Cars would rust into nothing, but before that animals would climb inside when it rained. Earth would teem with life, just not the life we thought it would.

It wasn't a bad thought. It was almost peaceful. Above me, a bird called and the song echoed down through the trees.

After we settled in, Johnson asked if we should repopulate the earth.

It got Adams choking and the rest of us staring until Adams' choking got pointed and Garcia started slapping his back.

"Isn't it our responsibility?" Johnson said. Even before our 80-year nap she'd been like this. The youngest out of all of us, always striving for more. I think she was the only one who seriously considered it. Even when Adams and Hyung got together nine years in and Hyung's belly started swelling drum-tight, it was never a discussion of population. It was a discussion of how the kid would feel spending half their life alone after the rest of us passed on.

We never had to face it. We still don't know what did it, though we have a dozen guesses. Even if we did know, I doubt we could've done anything about it. She almost made it six months along. We buried her at the end of the garden and mounted an empty grave for what could've been a kid. I think it's another reason why Johnson left. It's definitely why Adams left, but he orbited back to us after just a few months. He always does.

I don't know why I'm writing this, honestly. Sometimes I picture a hand, which in some dreams is alien and some a familiar pink with five fingers. I picture the hand turning these pages, but it's a hundred times more likely that this notebook will sit on the bench. First it will gather dust, then start to rot. The plastic wrap will protect it for now, but there's time. Nowadays there's nothing but.

Six years into the new normal, we climbed however many flights of stairs and sat on the roof of a skyscraper. The sun was cresting over the edge of the city, and it flung everything into a low glow.

"I always wished I could've done that thing they always show in space movies," Johnson said, and we looked at her. "You know that scene – that shot of the astronaut looking out over Earth from space. Always wanted that, but the cryo pods put that dream down fast." The Terra mission had been her first and last glimpse into space.

The rest of us hummed.

Adams said, "It was the first thing I did when I was allowed to walk around in my first trip up. Went right up to the window and looked out. I think everyone does it when they first get the chance." He looked over at me, Hyung and Garcia for confirmation.

"It was really something," Garcia said.

I nodded. Beside me, Hyung was lying with her hands propped behind her head and her feet dangling off the roof. She winked when she caught me eyeing her nervously, then edged forwards until her calves bumped the lip of the roof.

Three years from dying, she said, "It didn't look like it did in the movies."

Four years from leaving, Johnson replied, "Yeah? What'd it look like?"

None of us ended up with an answer. Instead we looked out over the city, empty apart from us, and watched the sun go down over the skyscrapers.

You should've seen the world before we left it on the Terra mission. I don't do it justice. And sure, sometimes it was terrible. Sometimes it was filthy and depraved; sometimes you watched the news and had to turn it off and go lie down with calming music thrumming soothingly at the back of your throat; sometimes you couldn't hear your own thoughts over the traffic and people spilled coffee on you and kept walking without apologising. It could get deafening, the ugly of the world.

But it was really something, once. You could click a button and talk to someone on the other side of the world. People raved about how smartphones disconnected us as a species, but I never found that. I'd see someone on the train, phone in their hand: they'd be grinning down at a parent, a boyfriend, a best friend. Crowds billowed in constant rivers through the cities, but people stopped to hand change down to a mug in front of a cardboard sign. They met for movies and hugged over coffee and waved at buses. They held grocery bags, babies, scarves, baskets of grain. They stirred cream into their coffee and picked herbs from the pots on the balcony and said *I love you* into cell phones.

Seven billion lives heading in seven billion directions. Earth was really something.

Still is.

It's been nineteen years now, going on twenty. No-one has come for us and we have carved ourselves a piece of the world. We sometimes roam, one or two or all of us – but mostly, we gravitate back. I'm still holding out hope Johnson will walk in the front door one day. Maybe we'll catch a glimpse of her on a radio transmission. I don't care what news she has.

Every morning I wake and check my crewmates. I wander from room to room, where Garcia and Adams have left their doors cracked so I can look in easily. We can get sick of each other, but some nights we'll crowd into the same room and I'll wake up in a sleeping bag the next morning to their comforting duo-wheeze. Often one of them will sleep in a neighbouring house, but they'll always leave me a door cracked, a window left open.

Afterwards, I'll head back to give the animals their breakfast – homemade chicken feed, pig slop, meat for the dogs. The vegetable patch comes last. I'll examine whatever needs to be examined depending on the season: potatoes in the spring, broccoli in the summer, carrots in the fall. When the time comes, I'll re-seed.

In the cold months, the crew will come to help dig up the potatoes.

LOGISTICS

A.J. FITZWATER

Alls I want is a goddamn tampon. Is that so much to ask at the end of the world?

Yo. Name's Enfys. This is, uh, my channel as I wander in search of tampons and the meaning of life in what's left of Western Europe. Seems, I'm, um, immune to the phage. So far, so apocalyptic.

Not so good at, uh, this talking stuff, but this is as good a way as any since people aren't totally into face to face right now. Anyone could be a latent carrier. Plus, it's a way to feel less mad. Until I go mad from talking to myself.

Guess you're wondering about, um, this lop-sidedness. Welp, I was on the table in Stockholm getting chest reconstruction surgery when Calais went down in a blaze of glory. Surgeons panicked, sewed me up, left me half the person I should have been. Ugh. Scars itch. Can't feel my nipple. So that sucks.

So, why would you do a dumb thing like major surgery in the middle of a worldwide epidemic, I hear you ask. Well, no-one knew we were in the middle of anything coz the CDC said they had it under control. I thought, hey, mutant flesh-eating bacteria. It's like HIV in the 80s, or Ebola in '16, or the Monkey Flu in '21. We'll deal. Movie of the week in six months.

Didn't even know about Zero Point Jacksonville or population estimates until I left Sweden. By that time things were starting to make a bit of sense and everyone had a channel. Guess that's what happens when most your newsrooms are wiped out, huh. Half the world's population, gone. Just like that. Geez.

Ugh, this is turning into one of those "where were you when" things. I dunno, do you need to hear mine? Everyone's had it rough and lost people. I don't have it near as bad as others. I wanted to do something different. Coz, need, and I can't be the only one, right? So.

SHOW ME THE TAMPONS.

Seriously. The African co-op did great work collecting and warehousing goods before everything north of the equator was sent up in smoke by those WHO idiots, but they could have left something behind in the emergency caches for those of us who are the subset of still wandering and still bleeding.

Anyway. I'm heading south through Germany. No, I won't put location tags on. Message me. Point me other channels. Help me out here please. Leaves in my undies is uncomfortable.

Enfys out.

* * *

...mazed anyone saw it considering ... oh, it's going now? Uh, hi again. Enfys still on the search for sanitary products in the afterlife.

So, um, thanks for watching. It's nice to know you're out there. The last people I spent meat time with was the lift I got from Malmö and they dropped me off in Hamburg. Well, what was left of Hamburg. Wall of smoke started freaking them out.

As for suggestions on where to find me those sweet sweet tampons. Someone said "try a roadside cache", and yo, were you even paying attention? Next cache I find I'll record so you can see what us wanderers are up against.

Dionysus365 – yo, sup – said resource crews were still scouring what's left of Berlin and there were untouched pharmacies buuuut I was too late. Smoke cloud over the city is huge. Tried to flag down one of the road trains but when they're on full auto nothing stops them until they hit the Mediterranean. And I can tell you straight, burn and resource crews have been ordered not to pick up stragglers outside the evac zones.

Not that I mind. I do not want to become a lab rat. I've seen the channels out of Joburg and Lagos. The sweet afterlife, just so long as you're cool with being the face of the biological resistance. Ugh. I'm no good with needles.

Annnd I have the idiots who were calling me the "titless wonder" and a few other choice things. Screw you. Guess it was too much to hope the apocalypse would wipe out all the jerks. I wanna make some joke about putting the facist into fasciitis. Ha. Nazholes. Ha!

Whatcha gonna do? Come looking for me? You're too bloody chicken, all locked up in your bunkers until the time is ripe to re-emerge.

I think it's awesome how the apocalypse didn't happen like all those sci-fi books predicted. All that dire-as shit preppers went on about was basically the only way they figured they could get women to worship them. "You'll come running when you need a man to REALLY protect you from the looting and pillaging and raping." Bish, please. That had been happening worldwide for time immemorial ANYWAY, and people have always been resisting that shit. We were always ready. If not ready for this.

So, the ones holed up in nuclear bunkers or their castles or vacuum-sealed mansions. One latent carrier in there, and PWNT!

Also, newsflash. The phage can wait you out.

Yeah, I've been watching some of the science channels. Can go dormant in stone? That's some weird ass shit. Eesh. The smoke cloud over Russia alone will probably trigger a nuclear winter.

Here. See that? It's summer yo. But all the insects are like, NOPE, and it looks like a billion volcanoes or thunderstorms all at once. And my hair is not streaked from stress. Ugh. Regular reminder: clean ash off with water, keep your eyes protected.

At least they thought to leave filters and face masks in the caches, eh. It's not so bad. Some places are clearer than others.

Uh, Go Oyo wants to know how I survived post-op in Stockholm coz it burned quick. That's … I don't wanna tell you that one right now. It's nothing like axes to zombie skulls or whatever. Just. It's fresh. Maybe later.

And BullaB from the new Caribbean republic – PR, sup – wants to know what an enby with a Welsh name and a Kiwi accent was doing in Sweden. Welp, two of those were choices, I moved there for capital R reasons. And hey, it also meant with my current immunity my life expectancy just went up. Loss-win. Dark humour, I know.

Anyway, it doesn't matter now.

Okay. Done for now. Tired, and air quality ain't great. Been walking for, uh, weeks. Fuel reserves gone south, and most solar and electric vehicles too. But I'm coping. It's scenic.

Catch ya.

* * *

…documenting the landscape before it's taken over by triffid wildlife. I mean, look at this. I call it: Death of the Front Lawn Brought on by Neoliberal Collapse of Worldwide Health Systems. Beautiful.

Um, comments. Captain Spike – hi – says there's a place for me in one of the enclaves in, um, maybe Joburg or one of the central cities. Oh my god, the afterlife even has drag queens. Thanks, love. I appreciate the thought, but I'm taking my time, sussing out the new world order.

The continent is big. Seriously, yo, Africa's not a country. Takes time to get around. Things are in flux. Too many people on the move. Too many tribal and community conflicts to re-solve. Central co-op doing the best they can, but it's still early days. Not even worth doing the census, if you ask me. They make it sound so normal, it's weird.

And we don't know the vector of the phage. Another wave could come at any time and then and it'd be Zero Point all over again.

Hey, does anyone have links to channels from California, or people formerly thereof? I know the whole country is basically wasteland, and the resource trains are programmed for Panama southwards but there's some, um, people … yeah, uh, put it in comments.

So, I said I'd, uh, show you a roadside cache. They're reg-ular but on the small side since wanderer stats are apparently low. Most people are pretty good at keeping to themselves. I've watched a few other wanderer channels, especially that one by the anonymous Bush Cook, and yeah, it's mainly true. You put up a flag and they'll leave some cooked food or supplies out for you. I've only come across one camp who were, like, totally strict quarantine and walked me off, no hassles, no fuss, they were nice about it.

Then there was a Roma camp who let me stay over. Was nice to have a bed for a few nights, but it ended up feeling weird being around so many. Nice people, they know how to survive.

So, um, this is a cache. They're kept in these new hybrid plastic units. Water proof, vermin proof, and, uh, supposedly phage proof. Apparently, this stuff could last a thousand years in outer space.

You'll usually find them near motorway off ramps or the site of an old landmark. They're flagged and people have been good about geo-tagging them.

It's kept unlocked, coz, come on. It's not survival of the fittest. It's simply the survival of. Good array of tinned and dried food, utensils, solar chargers, and a solar plate. So much better and cleaner and lighter than a gas cooker. Plus, for the days when it's, uh, overcast, they've gone for a wide range of accessibility. Like electric-based gear. Grid's still on, which is cool, eh. That's if you can find a handy outlet.

Always useful medical supplies, painkillers and such. No antibiotics, I mean, come on. This is the post-antibiotics world. Nappies and formula, good job there. Masks, wet weather gear, pet food, toilet wipes. But ... whaaat! Some goddamn sanitary pads. Enough for a couple periods anyway. This has gotta be a first. Thank you, um ... See Ay Gee. That stands for ... ah, there it is: Centralised African Government. Not to be mistaken for the former Central African Republic. Huh, the alliance vote must've gone through. I was paying attention to the South

American Alliance voting over the weekend, coz I got friends down in what used to be Argentina. If I can find them. Not that I'd get over there. We got super plastics outta this thing, but not easy ways to get across oceans right now.

Thanks for the comments and support, by the way. I appreciate you're watching someone rambling across Europe griping about tampons. Salonga82 said a tampon factory has opened in Lagos, and India is doing good things producing pads in rural areas on the back of their cottage industry. That's really cool. Just gotta figure out distribution models, yeah.

And since this is the afterlife, and I don't give a flying rat's, I'm putting it out there: I've received death threats from the nazholes. Ugh, you have no idea how hard it was to say that. Some old habits die real hard. Anyway, I've reported them to channel admin, and they're investigating, so that feels like progress. Thanks to BackChannelNinja from Oceania for hooking me up with the admins. Oceania is hanging on. They may be small, but they're mighty. Aroha nui, whānau.

Well, I have baked beans, sausages, and chocolate milk powder, so I'm set for a feast and a not entirely uncomfortable night's sleep. Imma go change my leaf for a pad. Oh my god, heaven.

Oh, and have you peeps watched the recording of Black Friday Live for Life in Luanda? That shit rocks! So awesome to see 3 of the 4 band members survived. Link is below.

Enfys out.

* * *

...course not every town and minute village has been sectioned. Gonna take years to develop proper testing procedures for the dormant phage. I mean, we lost a good chunk of the scientific and medical community coz many of them were first responders.

Huh. Wow.

Um.

So yeah. You're gonna find people still living in small pockets. They're usually good about sticking to quarantine rules and stay in touch with resource teams. No, I haven't seen any marauding bands. This isn't some sick HBO hellscape, yo.

And, no, I'm not gonna be ghoulish and show you an abandoned town still waiting for the burn crews. Cremation teams have done their best, but yeah, there are still bodies out there where they dropped. You can smell it. Those idiots who ran corpse hunter channels. Tsk. Really? Thought they were latent, but in the end it only showed the good side of chaos had them fooled...

* * *

SHIT.

Ha ha. Phew. Just a door banging in the wind.

Woah, weird. Empty. No quarantine signs. No bodies. Nothing. Interesting. Never seen a building made out of the super plastic before. Just. A regular house. Knew they were being experimented with before ... uh...

Listen. Can you hear all the birds? Insects too. Wind in the trees. So loud. Mmm, smell the fresh growth. Love it.

* * *

INT: Dark screen

[Unintelligible fast whispering]

* * *

...have half a chest and my goddamn binder tore and nothing fits shit shit shit...

* * *

...and with a bit of sticky tape like so, it does the trick. I mean, hell, I can find sticky tape in the afterlife but not sanitary products? Ugh. I know. What I'd give to have my implant reupped but that would, um, mean rejoining civilisation and my med papers are not all that since I left Stockholm in a hell of a hurry.

Yeah, so some of you have been asking about that. The whole hospital deal, a nurse having my back, er, front, ha ha. Those first weeks were, um, yeah.

But I then I got to thinking. She deserves her name out there, coz she was a goddamn hero like all those other first responders. Maybe she has family that doesn't know what happened to her. So anyway, here goes.

Phewf.

Her name was My. Here's a stealthie I took. I know, not entirely legal, but I didn't want her memory lost.

I didn't come round til I was in ICU, which wasn't necessary for my circumstances, but necessary for the circumstances. My and a few others put us in quarantine under the impression this would pass in a few days.

I mostly slept through the first European wave like some *Sleeping Beauty 28 Days Later* kinda crap. One of my drain sites got infected and I could barely sit up. My didn't lie, she said it was bad and that people were being evacuated and stuff was burning all over the place. I saw some of it on the internet, but connections were sporadic, information distorted by panic. The power wasn't on auto by then, like, not fully switched over to the Saharan solar or offshore turbine grids.

I dunno. I wasn't scared. Maybe coz she kept us on the happy stuff. End of the world was pretty boring, really.

My was real careful. Hazmat suit and quarantine procedures at all times. One of the other patients was mobile and would deliver us food and meds and stuff. I, um, kinda don't remember the others' names. I was in this weird place. I dunno, more annoyed that I only had half my chest realigned than thinking the world was coming to an end. I thought it would pass. We're humans, we're incredible, we're on our way to Mars. Shit, I wonder what's happened to them? Yeah, we can deal with one stupid flesh-eating bacteria that kills in 48 hours, right?

Huh.

It was obvious when the other nurses and doctors stopped coming. But My, she was doing great. I really thought she was going to make it through. She was so careful.

Last I saw her she had one of those purple blotches on her face. She couldn't hide it. Didn't really want to. We were all reasonably mobile by then, so she, uh, gave us packs and pills.

Then she turned up the gas and torched the place with her in it.

We were well away, but I heard the hospital go up like the bombing runs in Washington and New York and Seattle.

I guess we were the last out.

Um, so look at this view. Beautiful, huh. All those untended vineyards. What a waste. Mmm, and the sound of the river, so nice. Noticed waterways are coming back quicker than expected…?

* * *

Okay, I admit, I'd been holed up for a few weeks. That plastic house, okay? I didn't record from inside, coz, well, old habits. You think all the shitheads would figure we gotta work for the betterment of humankind, yadda yadda, but nah. They're quite happy to see this as the Second Coming or whatevs. Nazholes like cockroaches, still up in my mentions. Piss off. You're all cowards, stuck in your bunkers. And whatcha gonna do? Who's saving the world? That's right. The CAG. South American Alliance. Oceania. India. They put up with your goddamn colonial shit for hundreds of years and yet they opened their arms and their borders when it came to the crunch time.

Borders. Damn. Even thinking about such a concept now is so weird.

So yeah. I faked it when I channelled before. But now I'm on my way again. The ferries are running regularly to Alexandria, but. I dunno. The CAG is supposed to be the new enlightenment. Everyone has a place. But, do they really? I'm a cynic. I don't expect humankind to change that quick. Ugh, old habits old habits old habits. And I know the Big S has hit the more vulnerable people. My people. It's that old holdover. You wanna be in control of your death when you didn't have much control over your life.

I'm out of tampons again. Surely someone's got it together with sanitary product distribution? I mean, getting the word out and drone drops wouldn't be such a biggie.

Oh, thanks for all the concern when I was a little quiet on it. BigWiggie224 wants to know if I've been able to track down my fam in New Zealand. Still working on it. I buried enough of them Before it shouldn't hurt...

* * *

INT: Dark screen
[unintelligible sobbing]

* * *

It's the end of the world as we know it, and I feel fine, except for cramps and leaks and constipation.

Been a few months off my implant now, and my cycle is, um, reinforcing itself in style. Hard enough without my anti-anxiety meds. But now the dysphoria is real, yo. Stupid body.

Woah. A thought. If I'm dealing without my meds, what about those with chronic conditions. Insulin and dialysis and stuff. Dang, that's scary, yo. Hope CAG is onto that shit. I should look it up.

Hmm. Sea is pretty today. Some sunlight. Keeping on the move gives me something to do. Whoever is working hard at Google Maps is a goddamn legend.

Hell, what am I doing? Have I got a story for you!

I shit you not, but I met Jaybee Middlewake the other day. Totally hot even without the eyeliner. I'm not lying! He didn't want to go on camera, coz the art of celebrity is dead in the afterlife. And good riddance to it too.

He was working with an evac crew, and I joined in for a while coz it felt good to be doing something. Hells, incredible they let me stay with my shitty med papers.

The others from Black Friday were there. Inch said she'd seen some of my channel. I dunno, maybe she was just being nice. Justice gave me some moon cups. What a babe. I didn't tell her I can't use the things, they give me the creeps. I didn't go all fanperson tho, and freak out about how awesome the Luanda show was. This is the afterlife. I have to be cool with whatever it throws my way, even if it is my favourite punk band wandering out of the French mist.

But Jaybee. He was ethereal. This big team was evacuating an assisted living facility and some rest homes. I mean, what sort of jerk leaves disabled people behind in the afterlife? Thank god it wasn't a town the burn crews had been through. The place was pretty rank, but somehow the majority of them had survived this long. Turns out a couple of those kids were really handy at scavenging, and a couple of the older ones were really good cooks. They had running water, and they did their best.

I'm no saint. I admit I didn't think about it, like the meds thing. Makes me a damn regular jerk. Glad there are people out there with longer vision than me.

After we got them on a transport, the crew spent another couple days repurposing supplies from around the area. The hospital was a no go, already burned down. But there were some supermarkets and pharmacies, which were a gold mine.

It was … nice. Hard work. But nice. I'm not one to kiss and tell buuuut … believe me, don't believe me, up to you. Jaybee lost his whole family back in California, and his best friend from the band. We all need a bit of comfort in these dark times. I'd forgotten what it was like to hug someone. Bit weird, being lopsided. Ha.

Jaybee and me discussed a couple things. Like the trouble I've been getting up in my mentions. I said, I'm fine. Sure. There's been a couple nazhole stalker channels, but I'm pretty sure they're fake.

The other thing was the offer of joining the evac caravan to the ferry. I said, my grrl, my papers would not get me across the Mediterranean. He said, like some of you others have, they're working on a point of transfer test for everything from latency to actively involved. Actively involved, god, what a euphemism for something that'll kill you in forty-eight flat.

I dunno. You're talking to someone who's had a body stared at and prodded all my goddamn life.

But Jaybee was cool. He understood. He said if I ever make it to Lagos to look him up. How did the embodiment of modern anarchy come to be a CAG guy? Keep rocking on, my grrl. I hope you stay immune.

So, I'm heading thataway, away from the smoke. Thought I'd check out what Monaco looks like empty. I hear all those gold toilets are a trip if you can slip past quarantine...

* * *

Shit. And we're live.

Sorry for the whispering, but...

Okay, I was a jerk. I was fooling myself. Said I was cynic, but I guess this whole change thing has made me part optimist too. It was nice to slide through the world with my only problem being finding tampons, finding my next meal, and dealing with my meat sack. I wasn't hurting anyone.

Guess that's not good enough for some.

Shit, hang on.

Sorry it's so dark. It's like, 2am. But I've been moving all night coz there's someone out there.

Don't expect anyone to be round coz I've never done live before and shit I know I'm babbling but I can't stop. There's *someone out there.*

Shit, how do you turn location tags on. *Shit.* Sorry. Don't have a selfie stick. Ugh, shut UP, Enfys.

I don't know if they suck, or they just got on the good side of chaos. Not a roaming pack. They're pretty insular. Not cannibals or anything.

…

Shit. You heard that, right?

I think they've got guns. I know the new co-ops are doing their best to round up and dispose of weapons coz the afterlife isn't gonna be like that but there's only so much people can do and shit there are still nukes out there oh my god…

Shit shit shit shit I think I can see them. Not very stealthy but I guess what does it matter? Playing at First Person Shooter they don't care. Shit shit I'm in the middle of nowhere. There's a burn out a couple of kays back and a quarantine about five kays down the road but I don't think I'm fast enough, and the electric scooter I borrowed in Monaco is out of juice and like that would outrun a bullet, ha, shit…

…

I'm screwed, I stayed at the plastic house too long, got too comfortable. All cosy apocalypse. Ignore the stench, the smoke, the hunger, it'll go away.

Oh but Enfys, you say. Shouldn't you shut the hell up? They're gonna hear ya. What's it matter? A bullet, the phage, an infected scratch coz antibiotics are so last century. God, my scar itches. What's one more death out of three and half billion?

Shit ... can you hear that?

What the hell ... they've got drones? Of course they have. Well, unless a drone can open a dead refrigerator. Ugh, it stinks in here.

What, I ... can't hear what they're ... Christ, I'm not the praying type but if anyone's listening...

Oh god.

...

Oh god!

...

They're close.

Congrats Enfys, you're gonna be famous. Channelling live, from inside the fridge, it's death!

Shitshitshitshitshit...

...

The hell?

...

Uh. Huh? Someone's ... live commenting. They say ... they're in control of the drones and the nazhole stalkers are neutralised? Sure, Jan. How did you know they were there?

...

They're part of an online task force and were ... monitoring the nazhole's channel ... and saw me come online at the same time and ... cross referenced location tags and IPs ... and Jesus Christ on a biscuit, that's some top level chaotic good luck.

Nazhole that confident, huh?

Nah, yo. I'm not that dumb. I need a sign of good faith. How the hell some drones take down a nazhole with guns? Trank darts? That's some James Bond shit, yo. What's to say you won't use them on me? You ... need tampons, too?

* * *

INT: Dark screen.

[Quiet sobbing]

* * *

Gidday, yo, and welcome to the channel of the, uh, Tampon Express. Just doing final checks before we head out on the second ever delivery round. Mmm, the smell of fresher salt air, only slightly tinged with smoke. This time we're going up the eastern Mediterranean coast, heading into Gaza, then up into the former Aegean states and around the Adriatic. Map and distrib points linked below.

Course, it's not just tampons. Me and a few others worked hard to get those sorta things included in the medical supply drops. And here we are, round number two. Team Tampon kicking it, communal styles.

Uh, TikTakSinceBefore asks why I'm so obsessed with lady luxuries, and aren't there more important things to worry, don't we have bigger phages to fry? First of all DikDak, not everyone who needs sanitary products are ladies, so piss off. Second of all, we all do what we can, where we can. Right now, I care about tampons and gynaecological health for all sorts of genders, coz it's still HEALTH and it's one small thing I CAN do. You not learned anything from the Purple People Eater? Infections, pain, prolapse, endo, fibroids, menorrhagia. Yeah, ew, not ew. Those are all still happening, even if you don't want to think about the half the pop, no it's now sixty percent, it's happening to. Comfort, dignity, uh, people who bleed deserve that, even in these trying times.

Um, been hanging out for this trip, tell ya. Time off gave me a chance to brush up on the basics of a few other languages. Few weeks at the Alexandria outpost was nice enough, but it's not Addis Ababa, since Alexandria was cleaned out good in proper in one of the first waves. And um, thanks everyone for asking, I'm healing nicely after the surgery, and it's, uh, certainly a weight off my chest. Yeah yeah, shuddup.

Oh, need to tell you that new sexual health clinics have opened in Nairobi and the Dar es Salaam outpost. Dar es Salaam is the second newly opened filter point for refugees coming in from the latest phage wave in India, check the link for the refugee news channel below. Um, both these new clinics are available for IUDs, implants, oral birth control, and all your disposables. South Shore Hospital in Lagos has a full gynaecological suite. So glad it's up and running again. Desperately needed.

Oh, and I got a new implant too. I'm period free for years! God, it feels so good. I can feel the, uh, proper shape of me now.

Another reason I'm stoked for this supply run, other than getting out on the road, um, sea? Is that I'm finally gonna meet Minette in Gaza! Yeah, yo. The woman who saved my arse back in the ruins of Marseilles. Hey, Min, you bad arse, lookit all I got for you. Woosh. TAMPONS.

Yerp, links below if you're interested in her tutes on how to build and fly drones. Totally looking forward to getting flying lessons from her. The ex-military people here are cool, but they're too busy to teach a civvie how to fly drones just yet.

But it's, uh, getting kind of an imperative since I've been working with CAG Distribution on how to do supply drops without using up resources like the planes and boats that get first dibs on the rationed fuel stocks. But yo, necessity is the mother of invention, and Armageddon has been a great kick in the arse to divest humanity of fossil fuels. Check out the link to Doctor Samanat Apour's channel about the labs investigating that new dry fusion. It is mind blowing, yo.

Anyway, uh, rambling again. Um. What else? Oh yeah, if I'm back in time I can join the team heading up to the Svalbard Vault and do supply drops along the way. Pretty freaking cool CAG Medical discovered the phage doesn't settle in stone in extreme temperatures. Yay, the Sahara. Yay, the North Pole.

And, so cool, so many of the Sami way up North have survived, just like the Inuits out of Canada. Those people got survival skills, yo. Great to hear from them finally. Medical is still trying to figure out why certain genetic predispositions and indigenous people are more resistant to the phage. I know there is Māori ancestry somewhere back in my history my adoptive parents never wanted to talk about.

Do I know if my parents are still alive? Uh, don't care.

Heard from some fam who made it across the Tasman to the Melbourne outpost, though. Well … shit. Excuse me. Need a tissue.

Anyway. Just about time to set sail. Weather's looking good. I'll be channelling in live each day at 1pm West Africa time. Time conversion app, yep, in links. I'm stocked to the eyeballs with tampons, pads, moon cups, sponges, washable organic cotton pads, knickers, bladder control pads et cetera. And if I don't have what you want, drop me a line, and I'll run it past Distribution. I'll be heading to the factories in Lagos and Luanda after Svalbard to see how production is going. Shout out to councillor Yemisi Ekundayo, who is part of the council. She's the woman, yo. Keeps me busy. Plus her egusi soup is the bomb.

This is Enfys, your host with the tampon most, signing off. Be well, yo.

THE BILLOWS OF SARTO

SEAN MONAGHAN

Jack Kaufman took another breath of the rich, thick atmosphere. It had the slightest acidic tang. Invigorating.

Nearing the cone's summit now, the air felt cleaner, the heavy humidity of the forested walls replaced by a drier coolness.

Still, he was puffing. He'd climbed too fast. He knew it. Around him the verdant caldera cliffs stood mute. Kaufman felt ensconced in a vast amphitheatre. One where gargantuan beasts might have once fought for the pleasure of an audience of millions. The hole in the Sarto's crust made an oval thirty kilometres on its long axis. Over two thousand metres deep. To the bed of the lake.

Here, on the upward slope of the saddle to Steele Cone, he was only eight hundred metres below the caldera rim. Plenty far enough.

Scoria and pumice crunched underfoot. His boots were beginning to chafe, but he didn't have far to go now. Kaufman stopped to rest.

"Water," he said.

From the shoulder strap, his backpack wound out the tube and he sipped. Cool and refreshing. He could taste the electrolytes the pack had added, but he didn't complain. He even thought of asking for a little air too, but he'd decided to do this unaided.

When he was younger he wouldn't have even worried. But then, when he'd been younger, he wouldn't have even considered coming.

The day before, on the caldera's rim, he'd had a mask the whole time. Here, the forest made the oxygen content richer. Or so he'd read in the guide pamphlet.

Do not try to make the journey in a single day. Ensure you bring a bathing costume so as not to offend those from other cultures.

Take plenty of water.

Ensure you have a communications pad.

Do not travel alone.

Sometimes pamphlets seemed overly cautious in their suggestions.

Taking another sip of water, Kaufman let the tube go. It retracted into its recess with a quiet snick.

High above, a raptor circled. The wide, long wings made it look like a flying carpet. Kaufman imagined it whisking him aloft and depositing him at the sinter pools.

He could see his destination above and ahead. The lip of the cinder cone was no false summit. He'd eyeballed it from the caldera's edge before beginning the descent. The first part of the journey.

The cone's trail described a near-straight thirty degree angle, at its steepest, from the higher part of the caldera's floor. Off-centre, the peak stood less than two kilometres from the end of the caldera wall's switchbacking descent trail.

The forest had surprised Kaufman with its lush thickness. Filled with leafy trees and ferns and vines, abuzz with insects from invisible to mouse-sized, flocking with birds decorated in feathers apparently painted by hand by Heckel or Klee, or any number of rich, blocky colour-obsessed artists. That new guy, Cruther. Great slaps of reds and greens and pinks.

One of the tree species had brilliant lacy crimson flowers. Thousands of them spangled the forest, almost like intentional decorations.

The caldera's ancient cinder cone brought him measured barren contrast. More like the slopes outside the caldera. Few plants struggled through the loose chips of aerated red and white stone.

He saw mottled grey-white lizards basking or darting after glossy black-carapaced bugs.

"Enough rest," Kaufman told himself.

He started walking again. With each step forward, he lost a quarter step to sliding. Even with a vague trail, the cinder cone's surface was little better than scree.

There was solid rock beneath the deep cindery overburden. The angle of repose was more to do with the solidified granite below.

That didn't help his climb any.

The raptor screeched. It darted off toward the caldera wall. Kaufman trudged on.

Do not overexert yourself.

Make sure you've left your travel plans with the Sarto Excursion Centre office in York Central.

Exchange greetings with other travellers. You'll enjoy your journey far more this way.

Kaufman hadn't met anyone so far. From the outset it had been his plan. Get off Earth. Find something new. Travel. Engage in convivial conversations with other travellers.

Meeting new people is the reason many come to experience Sarto's wonders. The stark beauty of the world gives all visitors something in common.

Kaufman kept on walking. Losing one step for every four.

Halfway. The slope at its maximum.

He stopped again. Turned to survey the caldera's forest. From this distance it seemed hazy. Pollen and bugs and other particles made the air somewhat translucent.

Small steam eruptions from Steele Cone at times can affect the atmospheric composition inside Williams Caldera. These are not dangerous, but supplemental breathing apparatus must be carried.

"Water," the pack said, sticking out the tube of its own accord.

With a sigh, Kaufman sipped. "You know," he told it. "Taking care of myself was half the reason to come out here."

It didn't respond, of course.

Kaufman closed his eyes and remembered the kids rallying around. Making sure he was all right. Making sure the household ran without Marion's constant attention.

Turning, he opened his eyes and started up the slope again.

Three quarters of the way.

Then, just a hundred metres left.

Seventy-five metres.

Fifty.

Ten.

He stopped.

Looked ahead. Almost there.

From this point he could see the edges of the pools. The level pinky-white rims, with their waxy curved edges.

Sarto's sun beat down. Past its zenith, but still strong. The caldera floor would be in shadow by 3pm local time. Steele Cone's summit would lose the sun before five.

He realised the western part of the floor had lost the sun already. It was later than he'd thought.

He was looking forward to that. Apparently the sky looked stunning from the pools.

Something squealed from behind him.

Kaufman turned. He half expected to see a cluster of independent teens. Some kids excited and faux-startled by a lizard or big bug.

Instead he saw another flying thing. As big as the raptor. At least.

It was below his level. Near the forest. Above the old tongues of lava he'd traversed from the trees.

The animal had white-yellow wings, with a black body below. It almost looked as if the two were separate. Like a rat hang-gliding.

It gave another squeal and turned, speeding away for the trees. Gone.

Kaufman nodded. He'd read a bit about Sarto's isolated ecosystems on his way out. He didn't remember anything about hang-gliding rats.

With a smile to himself, he turned and continued up. In a couple of minutes he reached the flat area at the edge of the pools.

Ahead of him the sides of the closest, lowest, stood like a nib wall. Water ran across, keeping the curved sides slick and moist. The water drained into the loose rocks of the surface. Kaufman saw where the siliceous material had built up on the scattered rubble. Knocked around by the casual tromping of thousands of tourists.

The lower edges were ragged, almost like rows of teeth. There were more colours there. Thick greens and oranges. A mix of rocky chemical colours and lively algae and fungus.

As Kaufman strode across, the sound of his footfalls changed. The crunching lessened and the ground felt firmer.

There were dozens of the pools. He'd seen an aerial photograph in the pamphlet. It looked like someone had dropped a box of rings. Various sizes, all overlapping and cycling outward.

Across the diameter they ran back in steps. Each perhaps a half metre high. Rising as if stacked up.

The pamphlet had explained it all.

Water leaching from the caldera lake has changed the nature of Steele Cone. Over millions of years the percolating water has forced its way up, slowly dissolving and recrystallising minerals, resulting in the natural construction of the pools.

Kaufman didn't follow the geology, but he understood the stark beauty.

He was actually glad to have it to himself.

The three hundred and sixty-nine pools at the summit cover an area of over one and a half hectares (almost four acres). The largest pool, also the highest, spreads over two thousand square metres. Swimming in this pool is not recommended.

Kaufman walked right up to the edge. Dipped his hand in.

Cool, but not cold. He knew the pools grew warmer toward the top.

Kaufman took another breath. Setting the pack down, he began taking his shirt off. The pack opened its upper pocket for him to drop his clothing in.

He debated keeping his boots on. He didn't know how rough the pools' bases might be. The pamphlet hadn't mentioned that either way. It would be stupid to cut his feet.

In the end he stripped naked. No way to offend anyone if there was no-one around.

With a crackling sound, the pack compressed and sterilised his clothing.

"Wait here," he told it. That, it understood. If anyone came by, it would send him an alarm.

Stepping gingerly, Kaufman climbed over the first pool's rim. The edge felt clammy against his hand.

Right away he felt a twinge from his foot. Just where the boot had worn a blister.

The pool's floor was smooth and nearly flat. Solid. He could feel the ripples and bulbous shapes of it against his soles.

With the water up to his knees he walked across the pool. He shivered. The water wasn't unpleasant, but it was well below body temperature.

As he approached the opposite rim, where the next row of higher pools stood, the water deepened. It came halfway up his thighs.

He heard a bleep from the pack. Turning, he saw that it had climbed to the pool's edge. The pack's exterior had changed to a mottled, shimmery look. Waterproof.

"Just wait," he told it. The pack was supposed to be helpful, but it wasn't expected to be like a loyal dog.

He realised that even though the pools stepped back, in reality each pool was on a slightly different level. The pool to his left was slightly higher, the one on the right slightly lower.

It meant there was a rim that reached right to the more central pool. Kaufman stood on the rim between and climbed higher.

The pools formed a vague spiral out from the giant central

pool. He was cutting across. He supposed some pilgrims followed around the spiral, making sure they stepped into each of the three hundred and sixty-nine.

The next pool was a fraction warmer. And a fraction deeper as he walked across.

He climbed again. Gaining a half a metre each time. Gaining about half a degree or so in temperature too.

Kaufman didn't expect to reach the biggest pool, but he did want to be higher up for when the sun dipped behind the caldera wall.

Three more pools and he began to feel the effects of the climb again. The pools grew warmer by bigger jumps too.

Unburdened by clothes and the pack, and excited by making it here, he had forgotten his weariness. Wasn't that supposed to be part of the reason for visiting? Becoming reinvigorated by the mineral cleansing?

Kaufman stopped climbing.

The pool he'd reached felt like it was about thirty-six or thirty-seven degrees centigrade. A bit over a hundred Fahrenheit.

Perfect.

Kaufman allowed himself to slip down. He relaxed.

Never a naturally buoyant person, he found himself floating more than he was used to. Kaufman lay back, toes pointing at the sky, face just above the surface.

The sky glowed. High streaky clouds formed feathery wisps. A faint hint of rainbow colours in a narrow curve. A circumzenithal arc. The pamphlet had mentioned those too. Ice crystals in the clouds, still days, the sun at the right depth.

To his left the huge black raptor glided.

The faint smell of sulfur tickled his nostrils. He felt free and weightless. Surges of cooler water bounced against his skin, making him tingle.

Kaufman swallowed.

It would have been great to have shared this with Marion.

Taking a breath, Kaufman tipped his head back. With a couple of side strokes with his hands, he slipped under the water. It tried to push him up again. His skin tingled.

After a moment of immersion, he allowed himself to rise. The pool wasn't really big enough for swimming. He splashed out, spluttering, and put his feet on the bottom. Wiped his face with his hands.

As he took another deep breath, he heard a quiet splash from nearby.

Kaufman looked around.

"Hello there," a woman said.

Kaufman turned. She hung at the edge of the next pool over. Just her head visible. A little surge of water rose across the rim and trickled the couple of centimetres down to his pool.

Early forties, dark hair, skin a couple of shades lighter than his own, thick nose and full lips. Crystalline blue eyes. Almost white.

"I startled you," she said. She put her arms up on the pool edge, elbows out, and rested her chin on her hands.

"That's all right," he said. Aware of his lack of a bathing costume, he turned his body and held his hands down.

She grinned, showing white teeth, the right incisor fractionally crossed over the left. "You're overly modest."

"I apologise," he said. "I thought I was alone."

"Apparently not. I'm Kaz."

"Hi." Kaufman didn't know what else to say. He felt very

exposed. The surface reflection and water's refraction would hide detail, but not the obvious fact of his nudity.

Kaz smiled. She blinked, glanced at the caldera wall and back at him. "And you are?"

"Kaufman. Jack." He leaned forward. The water tried to bring him to the surface again. "I mean, just Jack."

Kaz held her right hand out. "Well, fellow swimmer, it's nice to meet you. Kaufman Jack, just Jack."

After a moment, when he hadn't moved, she said, with a grin, "You could shake my hand in greeting. After all, meeting new people is a reason so many come for the experience of Sarto's wonders."

"Really?" Kaufman didn't move. The phrase sounded familiar. Pat.

"Yes," she said, still grinning. "Sarto's stark beauty means all visitors have something in common."

"You're quoting the pamphlet."

She laughed. A watery, bright sound. Almost like something composed.

"Are you making fun of me?" he said. "Because I'm naked?"

Her grin faded. "I wouldn't dream of that. But if you've read the pamphlets, you know that clambering up here and splashing about nude is frowned upon."

"I read that."

"Other travellers might be offended."

"They might," he said. "I apologise. I'll call my pack and..." Kaufman trailed off.

Kaz had turned away.

She stared into the sky. Kaufman looked up, following her gaze.

He saw another one of the hang-gliding rats. A poor description, he thought. The airborne animal was a couple of hundred metres off. Moving along parallel to the caldera wall. Beyond, the lacy crimson flowers stood out against the green.

The animal's black body hung from the flowing white wing by a thick, blended trunk, with numerous stringy tendrils reaching to all points of the wing.

It moved with a slow, rippling motion. Like waves starting out from the centre of the wing. Rolling to the tips.

The body had a dozen or more short legs. It might have had a head like a bat's, but at this distance, Kaufman couldn't quite make out any more detail.

Kaz kept watching it. "Billow," she said. "I was starting to think I'd never see one."

"I saw one earlier," he said. "What are they?"

Kaz didn't reply. The billow kept moving, drifting away. It had passed them by and was losing altitude.

Kaufman considered taking the opportunity while Kaz's head was turned away. He could escape the pool, climb lower. Go and retrieve his tacky bathing costume from the pack.

He imagined her turning as he got one leg over the rim. Worse, finding himself slipping and exposing himself.

He stayed where he was.

Kaz turned to him. Moved to the same position with her elbows out, chin on her hands. She grinned.

"You're enjoying my predicament, aren't you?" he said.

"You didn't know about the billows, did you?" she said.

"Not until I saw one."

"Best-kept secret," she said. "Not many people come through here at this time of year. Sarto's seasons can be extreme. Higher angle of inclination than Earth's, but also the slightly eccentric orbit. With some precession and so on."

He did remember that the star was colder than Earth's sun, but Sarto was much closer. Orbited in just a few months. Rapid seasons.

"I read all that," he said. "Astronomy's not my strong suit."

"What is?"

"Embarrassing myself publicly."

She laughed again. Longer and fuller. Her whole face bright and joyous.

"You should come on up here," she said. "I'm wearing less than you."

"Oh." Right away a cascade of thoughts tumbled around his head. He felt even more embarrassed.

Bad enough to be naked, but to be so together with a naked woman. Out in the wilds. Alone. In a hot pool.

He would feel awkward.

Especially thinking still of Marion.

And the kids. What would they think? Their old man out here gallivanting in the hot pools.

Grown now, they had their own lives. Sherilee with her landscaping business, Caleb with a second baby on the way.

He'd barely seen Caleb since Marion's funeral. Sherilee called Kaufman every other day. Checking how he was.

Each of them had their own way of dealing with loss.

"It's not erotic," Kaz said now. She wore a wry grin. "The billows? You really don't know?"

"I read the safety and general information pamphlet," he said. "And the maps. But not much else. I just needed to get away. I liked the idea of a pilgrimage to these pools."

He found his hands relaxing. No longer covering his groin.

"The billows are the strangest local fauna," Kaz said. "You will have seen lots of animals and plants that are like things on Earth."

"Lizards," he said. "And the trees. Different, but yeah, it's like going to Europe and seeing other species."

"Butterflies," she said. "I was so used to red admirals and white cabbage butterflies that when I saw a blue morpho in Guatemala I just about fell to my knees."

"Monitor lizards did that for me," he said.

"But," Kaz said. "The billows are something else entirely. Something for which there's no analogue on Earth."

"Really?"

"Maybe ballooning spiders," she said. "You know when some species of baby spiders leave the nest. They feed out a strand of web. Let the wind catch it. After a moment there's enough web that the air lifts the baby away from the nest. The little spider drifts on the wind. Hopefully it lands in a tree somewhere and begins catching insects."

That didn't sound to Kaufman much like the hang-gliding rat. He told Kaz.

"Hang-gliding rat?" she said. "That's funny."

"I'm a funny guy."

"Now you're flirting with me? I should warn you."

"I'm not flirting," he said. "I'm *meeting other travellers.*"

Kaz laughed. "The billows are sort of mammalian. Live young, milk glands. Live on the ground. Standard four-legged skeleton, but they also have six musculature legs. They kind of crawl around like centipedes some of the time."

"I love them already. Do they make good pets?" Kaufman

cringed. Now he was *trying* to be funny. Not a good look.

Marion would have cringed too. The kids would have rolled their eyes. He was glad they couldn't see him now.

As soon as he could escape, he was going straight back to his hotel and booking passage home.

Kaz blinked at him. "That was odd."

"Sorry. I'm feeling out of sorts here."

"If you came up here, we could both be as embarrassed as each other."

"Yep." Kaufman didn't move, save for his hand stokes that kept him upright. He hung in the water with his knees bent, legs partly up. The water was only a bit over a metre deep.

"Anyway," Kaz said. "The billows have spinnerets too. They take their web and weave the wing. They attach it to their body and take to the air."

Kaufman didn't know how to reply. Unusual alien lifeforms had been studied all over the thirty planets where humans had settled. The billow sounded interesting, but not too extraordinary compared to some.

Pahlavi had a kind of living rock. Holm had land whales. Saxks, under the binary Kalla I and II stars, had a catlike animal that spent half its life as a plant.

"Interesting," Kaufman said.

"You don't understand," Kaz said. "There are millions of them. Only here in Williams Caldera."

"Millions. I understand."

Kaz gave him a pitying smile. "Why did you come here then? At this time of year. Just to swim naked?"

"Personal reasons."

"Right."

"Sorry," he said. He felt more awkward than just from being naked. "I didn't mean to sound uninterested."

Kaz smiled, but it seemed a little sad. The smile didn't reach her eyes.

"I'll go," he said. He figured he could slip around to the next pool around the spiral, rather than heading straight back toward his pack. Less chance of slipping, or revealing himself.

"Don't," she said. "You should come and watch this."

"Watch?"

"This is what I meant," she said. "I've been waiting for days. They should all go soon."

"Days? In the pools."

"My skin feels great," she said. "But no, not the whole time in the pools. I do come up at this time most days. You know. For the sky."

Kaufman looked up. The icy clouds shone back at him. The shadows around the caldera walls seemed deeper.

"I have a small camp," Kaz said. "Just out of sight of the main path. Well, just a tent, really."

Kaufman knew that long-term camping was frowned upon. He was surprised that rangers hadn't come to evict her. Someone would have noticed that she hadn't returned to her hotel. Kaufman's hotel concierge knew that he would be back tomorrow evening.

"Now you're thinking that I'm breaking the rules," she said.

"I'm thinking that I'm glad to have met you," he said. "I wouldn't have known about the billow if you hadn't told me. Thank you."

Kaz stared at him, blue eyes intense. "You should come up here with me," she said. "I'm not going to jump you."

"I didn't think you would. And you're not worried I would try?"

Kaz shrugged. "You wouldn't." Her eyes glanced up. "Anyway. There are millions of billows. If they all fly at once ... well. That would be quite a sight."

"It would." Kaufman couldn't quite picture it. Millions. He could understand someone camping out to see that, though. "Why isn't this something on the Sarto tourist calendar?"

"Because these animals don't follow a calendar."

"So you don't know when this will happen?"

"Nope."

Kaufman stared at her. "So you'll just wait until ... how long have you been waiting so far?"

"Six days. I'm not obsessive."

"Six days." Maybe verging on obsessive, Kaufman thought. "When did it last happen?"

"No-one knows."

That didn't make sense. "Someone must know. Otherwise why would you be waiting?" He wondered if Kaz was mad. He might be in more trouble than he'd thought.

Kaz grinned. "It's a long story."

"I've got time." Part of him wanted to run away. Forget propriety and just race to his backpack. Get dressed and flee down the mountain.

Another part felt fascinated.

"Cool." Kaz blinked and watched him. "I'm not insane," she said. "I'm not taking medication for any condition, nor have I ever. I have visited a therapist, on two occasions. First when I lost my baby. Second when my sister was killed in a diving accident."

"I'm sorry to hear that," he said.

"Thanks. I'm sure you're wondering why I told you."

"Little bit."

"So as you know I'm in my right mind. Here's what I did. Last time I came out here, I saw them. The first day I saw just one. I fell in love. On the third day I saw a cluster of six. It was rapturous. Do you understand?"

Kaufman thought of Marion's expression when she saw the face of the advancing Franz Josef Glacier. That huge cliff of ice had made her tremble.

Not from the cold, but from the sheer scale of its glowing blue depths.

"I understand," he said. He'd never felt it himself, but seeing it in Marion had been enough.

He'd felt a vague touch of rapture himself simply watching her. That was a good memory of her. Far better than those days with her pallid face and all the tubes and incisions and serious doctor conversations.

Despite myriad advances – leaping between stars for one – sometimes people got sick and didn't get better.

"I looked up the satellite imagery," Kaz said. "From back in the old days. Before anyone got here."

"Okay." Every human-occupied world, outside of Earth, had been surveyed for decades before even the initial teams had arrived. All those quadra-whatever-trillions of pages of data and images were all public record. Easy enough to set up searches to find anything you were looking for.

"I wondered if they ever flew in bigger groups. And, oh boy, what I found!"

"Millions," he said.

"Exactly!"

"But irregularly?" He realised he'd allowed himself to drift closer.

"So it seemed. But I kept digging away. Turns out there is a cycle. Farthest distance from the star. High inclination. And the blooming of the lace trees. When those three things coincide."

Kaufman looked at the forest again. Hundreds of thousands of the crimson flowers. With the sun lowering, the flowers stood out even more.

"Now," he said.

Kaz took a breath, her nostrils flaring.

"I didn't see them," he said. "You said no-one knew. Why do they do it?"

"They hide. They're good at that. Believe me, I've looked. And no-one does know."

"Except you."

She gave an impish grin. "Because I went looking. Do you know how much research is going undone? Thirty inhabited planets."

"More."

"Yes."

"So you're a researcher? One of those post-docto—"

"Funny. I'm an artist." She leaned forward, peering at him, eyes wide. "I'm seeking inspiration."

"I guess you found it." Kaufman smiled to himself. He'd drifted almost right to her. As if he was a breath of air and she was drawing him in. Just the pool rim between them.

She breathed again. He was only a half metre from her.

"So what do you do? Travel the spiral arm?"

Kaufman laughed. "You'll hate it."

"Uh-oh. You're a real researcher. A post-doctoral fellow

studying xeno-fauna."

"I'm an art critic."

Kaz's hands darted out. She grabbed his shoulders. Her grin so wide it showed some of her upper gum.

Kaufman splashed.

"Favorite artist?" she said.

"Uh … Klimt?"

"Huh! Most loathed?"

"Caleb Cruther."

"It's perfect," Kaz said. "Come up here."

"I shouldn't." He could picture Marion, smiling, urging him on. "What kind of art do you do?" he said.

She let go of him. "Now, I'm not going to talk any more. I'm going higher. I'm going to see if the billows come."

She stood.

Kaufman saw that she had no breasts. Just two finger-length scars across her chest.

Reaching up, she grabbed the half-metre-high rim of the next pool. Moving toward the centre, she pulled herself over.

Kaufman stared out into the caldera's vast void.

He saw again those images of the thing growing and spreading through Marion.

Above, he could hear Kaz splashing through the water. He paddled away. Across to the edge of the pool. Looking down on the others he'd traversed.

His pack still stood on the edge of the lowest pool. Waiting for him to return. A loyal dog.

The lacy crimson flowers looked like lights. Christmas lights. Ready to shine out over the caldera as the sun slipped lower.

He saw more of the billows. A cluster of them.

Six.

Their webby wings waving in slow ripples. The animals must be light. Thin-boned, with body cavities.

They looked so perfect. They danced together. Swirling.

A vortex. A cascade.

A tumble of them, flitting and floating.

Kaufman realised he'd become entranced. He felt his breathing coming in gasps.

More billows emerged from the forest. Another cluster of six.

Family groups. Or mating ... groups. Not pairs. Hexa-somethings.

Not important.

Kaufman pushed away from the lip. He stood. Turned. Splashed across to the rim where Kaz had climbed away.

She wasn't in the next pool.

Nor the next.

"Kaz!" he called.

He kept climbing.

Three more pools. He saw ripples still reflecting from the flat edges. She'd come this way.

"Kaz."

Two more pools.

At the next he stopped and turned.

More and more billows joining the others. Dozens of clusters of six. Hundreds. More and more slipping from the trees. Wings unfurling. Taking flight.

It felt as if they would fill the caldera. They would sweep Kaufman up in their whirlwind.

Their squealing formed a loud backdrop. He heard a rhythm to it.

He kept climbing. Kept calling.

He found her another four pools on.

Kaz sat with the water up to her shoulders, her back against the far wall.

The last pool.

Around him vapour hung on the surface. The water felt tingly. Acidic. And hot.

Kaz grinned at him. "I heard you shouting," she said. "Thought you should stop that."

Kaufman nodded. Out of keeping with the event.

"I just…" he trailed off. Silence was better.

He strode through the pool toward her.

Kaz stood. Facing him.

"I'm…"

She put her finger to her lips. Turning, she climbed to the last pool.

Kaufman followed.

It was different. So wide, compared to the others. And no other level above.

Sinking down to his shoulders next to her, he could see the caldera all around. It was like being in the ocean, with a horizon.

He could feel the heat, too. Far too hot, but not unbearable. He wondered how long he could stay.

"See," she said.

Stretching down and out with his feet, Kaufman found he could not touch the bottom.

Instinctively he grabbed her hand. Kaz took it and squeezed.

They hung together, treading water. Looking down, the water seemed black. The wall faded to nothing.

He wondered how far it went down. In the centre he could

see ripples. The water boiling up from below. It would be very hot out there.

"Swim around." Kaz tugged on his hand.

Together they returned to the side. Kaufman mimicked her pose, elbows out, chin on his hands.

Below, the caldera continued to fill with billows.

Thousands. Tens of thousands. Now Kaufman felt as if he himself was flying. His body buoyant and tingling in the mineral water. The sweep of the wafting billows.

He didn't know how they stayed aloft. There were so many of them it seemed as if they would all jam and bump. Make collisions that would send them tumbling.

"Birds flock without crashing," Kaz said.

"You read my mind?"

"Really? No. I was just wondering how they didn't knock each other out of the air. And then I thought of birds."

Kaufman didn't reply. He watched the spectacle. He didn't know if he'd ever seen anything so astonishingly beautiful.

He bumped Kaz's elbow. Reached his hand across to hers. Took it.

She smiled at him. Pulled his hand underwater. They hung together, kicking gently, opposite arms on the rim, holding hands underwater between.

The sun kept moving on. Almost at the caldera's rim. The Western wall already falling into darkness. The crimson flowers still picked up the ambient light, glowing like stars.

Below, the spiral of mineral pools reflected the light. Shimmering with the slightest tremors. The calm affected by the movement of hundreds of thousands of billows.

Their numbers continued to grow.

"It keeps becoming more spectacular," he whispered.

"Yes."

"You were right. Thank you for sharing this."

"You seemed so sad," she said.

Kaufman swallowed. He turned to face her. "How could anyone be sad now?"

"Exactly."

With a grin she leaned forward and kissed him. A tap of her lips against his. She stared right at his eyes.

Kaufman trembled.

"This," she said. "This is my kind of art. Sharing this. Could it be any better?"

It couldn't, he thought. The wash and vibrance of colour and life. It felt mystical.

"Maybe," he said, "after this, we could travel together. For a while."

Kaz stared at him, surprise in her eyes.

"But you're an art *critic*. We'd just argue all the time."

Kaufman gave a subtle shake of his head. "If this is your taste in ... beauty, we'll never have—"

Kaz put her finger to his lips.

"Good," she said. "Yes, let's take a couple of days. I'd enjoy that."

Below, the billows continued to increase in number. The brilliance of their wings picked up the reds of the flowers, creating a vague pinkish haze.

Above, the clouds capped it all, with their streaky filigrees. Some edges burned a bright silver.

Somewhere in between, the wide-winged raptor still circled. Slowly. Its stark absorbent ebony formed a perfect counterpoint to the swirling all around.

"Thank you," he said. "This is what I needed."

Kaz squeezed his hand. "I think," she said, "it's what both of us needed."

Kaufman stared out. One day, thousands of people would want to see this. How perfect to see it now, like this.

With Kaz.

He knew barely a thing about her. But then, he knew that he knew her inside out.

A MOST ELEGANT SOLUTION
M. DARUSHA WEHM

I always said I wanted to be one of the first to die on Mars. I never wanted to be the last. But here I am.

I can't even tell the others apart now. I know that inside those vaguely undulating metal cocoons are the bodies of the rest of my team – Marshall, Cherie, Gem and Abdul. Which squirming ovoid contains whom – there's no way to tell.

And I'm about to join them. The swarm has already engulfed my legs. I can't feel anything below the knee, which is a kind of relief. Devoured by my own creations is a terrible enough way to die – at least it probably won't hurt.

I know I should be mourning the others, or desperately trying to save myself, but I don't feel anything like that now. Maybe this is a side effect of the paralysis, maybe it's not just a physical but an emotional anaesthesia. Because all I can think about is how I got here. How we *all* got to be here, lying on the floor of our brand new habitation buildings, smothered by tiny robots.

* * *

Abdul joked about grey goo, right from the beginning. We'd been living and working together in the lab on Earth for a year before we left, one of several teams preparing for the trip. None of us knew which team would be chosen to be the first, so we all prepared. Working with the bots was a core competency for everyone, since they were the lynchpin of the plan to make Mars habitable. But everyone knew that they were really mine. *Betsy's bots,* they called them. Except, of course, when Abdul was imagining them taking over the universe.

"That's not funny," Gem said. We were all scientists, so none of us were superstitious, exactly, but Gem never liked to hear talk of things going wrong. They always turned the conversation back to how to prevent disaster, instead of how to react to it.

Gem was a glass half full kind of person.

"That's where you're wrong," Abdul said, winking at Gem. They'd been flirting since day one and we all knew they'd probably end up a couple, whether it was on Earth or on Mars. "It's hilarious."

When the tiny bio-engineered bots had barely filled a Petri dish and were sprouting adorable models of habitation, sanitation and manufacturing facilities, it was kind of funny.

When we'd been on Mars for two months, living and working in the full-size versions of their creations, but they kept on replicating regardless of our programming, it stopped being amusing.

* * *

It's not as if none of us could have predicted the bots swarming and developing a plan of their own. We all thought about it, Abdul's jokes were just the most obvious way to describe the concern. Everything is a trade-off, and at the time it seemed like a reasonable risk in return for the things they could do for us.

Now, as they make their way up my legs, I think I honestly couldn't have done anything differently to prevent this outcome. But I do wonder if we should have spent more time planning for the worst-case scenario. I wonder if Gem, in their shimmering living coffin, had thought about that in the end.

* * *

"Okay, that's just freaky."

Marshall visibly shuddered as I let the bots crawl over my hand. They didn't really behave like insects, and they definitely didn't feel like insects. They were silky, almost warm, especially after a long stint in the desert in my suit. Thermoregulation in a suit is never right.

"It feels nice," I said, holding my hand out to him. He made a face and disappeared into his hydroponics lab. Marshall was always happier dealing with things that grew rather than things we built. He said he'd take evolution over engineering any day.

I chuckled and watched as a small cluster of bots gathered in my palm for a fraction of a second, then splintered off like a flock of birds dispersing. It was oddly beautiful.

We were still in our prefab shelter then, the modular building serving all our needs, albeit barely. I was just about finished with the final programming to let our bots loose, to let them begin building us a permanent home, using the elements already extant on Mars to create a form of protection from those selfsame elements. It was an elegant solution to an ugly problem, and I couldn't wait to see what they would devise.

I admit that I anthropomorphised them. Not individually, of course. I didn't come up with thousands of names or anything, but I thought of them as alive. Like working animals, maybe.

When I thought I was alone, I talked to them. After a while, I didn't care if I was alone or not.

It bothered Cherie. She took me aside one night after we'd all kicked back with a movie and asked if I was okay.

"Are you asking me as a friend or as my boss?" The five of us were a proper team, hashing out issues collectively, but there had to be someone with whom the buck stopped. A mission lead who, when the shit starts hitting the fan, could make a decision and know that we'd all carry it out, no questions asked. That was Cherie.

A shadow crossed her face as if my question hurt her, or maybe I was just imagining that. Projecting.

"Yes," she said, eventually.

I couldn't help but smile.

"Yeah, I'm okay," I said. "It's mostly rubber ducking. Look, I don't really believe they understand me or anything." I laughed. "They're way too small for verbal language processors."

She nodded, but I could tell she was still concerned. Rightly so, probably.

* * *

I'm not talking to them now.

I've never been claustrophobic – none of us could be in this job – but I think it's instinctual to be terrified of being smothered, buried alive. And yet…

They've got my hands now and the only thing I can still move is my head. I ought to be screaming, out of my mind in fear. But I've got a deep-down body calm instead. The bots are highly adaptable, able to fabricate all manner of compounds. The part of me that still feels things is inordinately proud that they have figured out how to control our bodies and minds as they do whatever it is they are doing. Breaking us down for constituent elements, I presume.

Amazingly, even that thought doesn't repulse me. They have done an excellent job.

* * *

The first habitation they built was impressive, though more for the proof of concept than for the structure itself: it had four walls and a roof, with airlocks and shielding in all the right places, but that was about it. It was functional.

"It's a bit ... boring," Abdul said, walking through the boxy rooms.

"It sure beats the prefab, though," Gem said, stretching their arms high above their head and utterly failing to reach the ceiling.

I couldn't keep the grin off my face. "It sure as shit beats the prefab," I said, not bothering to conceal the pride in my voice, "and that prefab wasn't the designer's first try out of the gate. This is." I ran my hands over the smooth walls, extruded by my bots after their own design. "And the next one will be even better."

"How do you know?" Cherie asked.

"Because that's what they do," I said. "They adapt."

* * *

The next buildings they fashioned were better, and the ones after that better still. It was becoming almost comfortable on Mars.

Not really, of course, we still needed airlocks and suits and we were drinking recycled urine, but it was better.

It wasn't just the buildings though. *They* were better. The bots themselves.

Adaptation. It's a survival mechanism in organic life, a result of the drive to continue being. Of course, it never occurred to me that it could work in reverse – that the programmed nature of my bots to adapt would lead to them possessing a drive to survive. I can only assume that's what's happened. I programmed them to do whatever they had to in order to make a habitable environment for us humans, but I guess the purpose got lost, mutated by the very adaptability that made them useful to us in the first place.

Maybe it's only fair that we are now becoming useful to them.

My sarcophagus encloses me completely now. I can see nothing, feel very little on my skin. Even my breathing and my heart rate seem to be slowing, but there's still no panic, none of that survival instinct left in me.

Thinking is slow. Like walking through a bog.

I ought to be afraid. I ought to have regrets and longing. I ought to think of home or family or lovers. I ought to wish I could see the stars.

But my only wish is that I could live to see what my children will become.

* * *

"Betsy?"

The voice comes to me as if from a long distance, and it's familiar and comforting, even though I can't identify it.

"She's coming around; give her some space."

There's a rustling and I become aware of light. I can see, though I can't seem to open my eyes. The light becomes stronger and shapes coalesce in my vision and I realise that what I can't do is *close* my eyes. I can't blink.

The strangest part is that it feels completely normal.

I try to take a deep breath but there's no fullness in my lungs, no weight to the air, only the incongruous taste of seltzer in my mouth. I don't even feel my chest expanding. I guess I'm not breathing anymore, either. Am I dead, yet somehow still aware? That doesn't seem plausible.

The shapes around me firm up and I recognise Cherie. Only, I don't recognise her at all. Her long hair is gone – not cut short but completely absent – and her skin is a covered in a black, scaly coating.

"Betsy," she says, her voice the only thing that seems close to my memory of her, "how do you feel?"

I think about the question. I remember the bots engulfing me, suffocating me, devouring me. But I haven't been deconstructed for my useful components after all.

Quite the opposite. I'm whole. More than whole – I am more. I can see infrared, taste radiation. I've been augmented. Improved.

"I feel … great."

Something like a smile appears on Cherie's face and she helps me up. We are still in the main habitation building, where I'd found the others being swarmed by the bots. The airlock opens – no, it's not an airlock anymore. It's a door. An Earth-style single door, through which Abdul enters. He's not wearing a suit. He's not wearing anything. Looking down at my own body, I see that the black scales are part of us. A kind of *permanent* suit, I suppose.

"Betsy – I'm glad to see you finally decided to join us."

"The ... others?" I ask, still unsure how to work my new voice.

"Everyone is awake, we are all fine," Abdul says, then his obsidian face slips into a grin. "Better than fine. Though, I have to say, this is going be awfully hard to explain to NASA."

I obviously look confused, so Cherie explains.

"You did a good job, Betsy. Too good, maybe. You programmed your bots to do whatever it took to make Mars a feasible place for us to live. And they did. They found a most elegant solution. They didn't change Mars to suit us. They changed us to suit Mars."

A BRIGHTER FUTURE
GRANT STONE

Samuel had been quiet the whole trip, but when Peter pulled the van into the driveway he gave a squeal of delight, jumped out and ran to the door. Then ran back and rapped on the windscreen. "It's locked."

"Course it's locked," Peter said. "There should be a key under a pot plant out the back."

Samuel ran off again.

"Looks nice enough," Lisa said.

Peter looked at the house. "It's new at least."

"You don't like it?"

"It's fine."

"Better than fine, little brother. It's a year's worth of free accommodation in the most expensive part of Auckland."

"Well, there is that."

Lisa opened the back of the van. "You going to sit there all day, or do I need to set up your new, already-furnished, free house all by myself?"

Peter walked through the front door to the smell of fresh paint.

Samuel shouted from upstairs. "I call dibs on the corner bedroom!"

* * *

It didn't take long to unpack, but by the time they'd got things sorted they were all exhausted. Peter went out for fish and chips and they ate them at the kitchen bench straight from the paper. Peter had worried that Samuel might be too nervous to sleep. But by the time dinner was finished he was already yawning and his eyes closed as soon as his head hit the pillow.

"Dad?"

Peter hesitated, his hand over the light switch.

"You're really good at looking after me. I'm glad you're my dad."

"I'm glad I'm your dad too, buddy. You're my favourite child."

"I'm your only child."

Peter kissed Samuel on the forehead. "Still counts. Now sleep. You've got a big day tomorrow."

* * *

Lisa had made them both a cup of tea. "Have you seen this?"

She handed Peter an envelope. Inside was a small card: "On behalf of all faculty and students, please allow me to congratulate Samuel Wilson on winning the Blake scholarship and welcome you both to the Saint Enoch family. Welcome to a year that will change your life."

"Well, that's nice, isn't it?" Lisa said.

"Yeah," Peter said. "It's just that after the last couple, I was quite looking forward to a boring, non-life-changing year."

Lisa put the cups on the coffee table. "Oh, honey. Come here."

I'm not crying, Peter told himself.

Lisa held him until the worst had passed. His tea was cold by the time he sat down and took a sip. He didn't mind. "I keep telling myself I'm over it," he said, "that I can move on. But it keeps hitting me when I least expect it."

"It's not either-or, little brother. You'll never be over it," Lisa smiled, "but you have to keep moving, for Samuel's sake. Coming up here is the right thing to do – a year at one of the best schools in the country. There's been, what, three Prime Ministers who attended Saint Enoch's?"

Peter snorted. "That's not necessarily a ringing endorsement."

"Come on. You're setting him up for anything he wants to do in the future, and it's what Melanie wanted. She applied for the scholarship, didn't she?"

"Yeah," Peter said. Melanie hadn't said anything to him about the scholarship as far as he could remember, but it was possible she'd mentioned it. She would have applied at the start of February and by the end of that month things were changing so fast Peter could hardly think. He had found the acceptance letter in a pile of bills on the coffee table in June, and by then he couldn't ask her. She was still breathing then, but only technically. The machines were doing all the work.

Peter blinked. Lisa had been saying something. "What?"

"Hurry up with your tea. It's not just Samuel that's got a big day tomorrow."

He tipped the remains into the sink. "Sure you won't take the bed? I don't know how much sleep you're going to get on the couch."

"I'm not kicking you out of your bed on your first night in the house. Anyway, the couch might be great and the bed terrible."

"Thanks for helping us get set up."
"We're family, little brother. It's what we do."

* * *

The sound of heavy shoes stomping down the stairs made Peter look up.

Lisa was already in the hallway. Samuel stood on the bottom step wearing his new uniform. The blazer was too big and his trousers flowed over his just-polished shoes like a robe.

"Christ, Peter," Lisa whispered. "He looks like a rich wanker."

Lisa wrapped Samuel in a hug that he grudgingly permitted. "You look so grown up."

"I look like a rich wanker," Samuel said.

"Samuel Aaron Wilson," Lisa said, "what kind of language is that? Be careful – I hear boys who talk like that get their mouths washed out with soap at Saint Enoch's."

Samuel looked frightened.

"Hey," Peter said. "Buddy. They don't do that. Aunt Lisa is pulling your leg."

"I know," Samuel said. The look on his face did not change.

* * *

"It's all boys. No girls at all."
"You told me you didn't like girls."
"When I was eight. I'm eleven now."
"So you like girls now?"
"You know what I mean. It's just weird, a whole school with no girls." Samuel looked in the rear-view mirror, twisting his tie.

"And I don't like this. Feels like I'm being strangled."

"You'll get used to it," Peter said. "It's good to know how to knot a tie. You'll need to wear one when you're out in the real world."

Peter had already driven past the school entrance three times, looking for a place to park. He'd seen a few gaps, but nothing big enough for the van.

"You don't wear a tie."

"I'm wearing one today."

"Today's different."

A BMW pulled out just ahead. An Audi on the other side of the road saw the gap the same time Peter did. He pulled in before the Audi could move. The van lurched to a stop. Something heavy in the back slid across the floor and crashed into the opposite wall.

It was nearly eight-thirty. The footpath on both sides of the street was a sea of blue blazers. Every other vehicle was black or silver, mostly Mercedes or BMWs. There were no other vans. Parked next to a cluster of Land Rovers was a red Porsche convertible. A balding man leaned against the driver's side, talking on his phone, nearly in the middle of the road. Nobody seemed bothered.

"Dad, I—" Samuel blinked, looked away.

"It's okay, Samuel. I get it. You're thinking this is a giant mistake. You want to go back to Thames, your old school, your old friends, our old life. The next few weeks won't be easy, but we'll get through. Before long you'll be walking around like you own the place."

"I know. I'm just scared, I guess." Samuel wiped a palm across his eyes.

Peter blinked. "Fear of the unknown is nothing to be afraid of."

"It's not that. It's just—" He gestured at the window. "I don't mind the new school, but I don't want to change. I don't want to change into one of them."

"That's never going to happen." Peter brushed a speck of dust from the shoulder of Samuel's blazer. "Just because you wear a rich wanker's uniform doesn't make you one. You'll always be you. You'll always be my boy."

"Dad! Language!"

Peter raised his hands, "Sorry, buddy. But it's true."

Samuel sniffed. "Thanks, Dad."

The bald man was still on his phone. He seemed to be staring straight at Peter, although it was impossible to tell. He wore mirrored sunglasses, the kind that always made Peter think of American cops.

Peter unclipped his seatbelt. "Come on then. Let's get in there and see what's so special about this school where you need to wear a tie."

* * *

Principal Bridwell met them at the door of his office

"Peter Wilson." Principal Bridwell wrapped Peter's grip in a fist like a shovel blade. "And this must be Samuel. Welcome to the Saint Enoch's family."

The wall behind Bridwell's desk was covered in framed certificates.

"How have you found Auckland so far? Getting used to the traffic? Quite a change from Thames, I bet."

"It's a bit busier, yeah." Peter found his mouth suddenly dry. He left school twenty years ago, got married, built a career and raised a kid. A memory surfaced: him and Martin Morgan in Form Two, waiting outside the headmaster's office. Waiting to be asked who threw Martin's bag and broke the window.

"And you're a builder, I understand?"

"I run my own company these days. Well, I did. I'm wrapping up a couple of projects back in Thames, and then I'll be looking for something closer. Although the way the property market is at the moment, going back to swinging a hammer might not be a bad idea." Peter realised he was waffling and closed his mouth.

"Indeed. And Samuel. I'm sure you're keen to meet your new classmates."

"Yes … yes sir." Samuel stared at his shoes.

"No sirs round here," Bridwell said. "I know we don't look it, but Saint Enoch's is a modern, progressive school. Call me Alastair, if you'd like."

Yes sir – I mean Alastair." Samuel raised his eyes up like he was looking at Father Christmas. Bridwell smiled.

Someone coughed in the doorway.

"Ah. Fullerton. Come in," Bridwell said. "This is Samuel Wilson and his father. Samuel's the recipient of the Blake scholarship this year."

Fullerton inclined his head. "Welcome to St. Enoch's." There was a smile on Fullerton's face, but it felt more mocking than friendly.

"Fullerton is a prefect in your year," Bridwell said to Samuel. "He'll look after you until you've got used to things. You're in the same homeroom. Speaking of which, you should both be there," Bridwell looked at his watch. "Now," he said at the same time as the bell rang.

"Come on then," Fullerton said, already halfway to the door. Samuel gave a backwards glance but by the time Peter opened his mouth to say goodbye both boys were gone. He thought of Samuel blinking back tears in the van fifteen minutes ago.

"He'll be fine," Bridwell said. "Fullerton's a good lad. His father attended St. Enoch's. His grandfather too. Fullertons are part of the fabric of the school."

"Yeah," Peter said, sounding more confident than he felt. "He'll be fine."

Bridwell leaned back in his chair. "I'm glad you decided to take the scholarship. Fullerton isn't the only third-generation student. It's good to see past pupils return with their children. But it's nice to get some new blood too."

Peter tried to smile. "We're happy to be here."

"There's a small social event in the hall this Friday evening," Bridwell said. "I'd be honoured if you could attend."

"I'll be there," Peter said. "We both will."

The street was nearly empty by the time Peter got back to his car. A crumpled muesli bar wrapper lay on the passenger seat, the remains of Samuel's breakfast.

* * *

Peter heard the front door slam, then footsteps on the stairs. By the time Peter followed, Samuel's door was already closed. Peter leaned in but couldn't hear anything. The door opened just as he raised his hand to knock. Samuel had changed into jeans and a black sweatshirt. His uniform lay crumpled on the floor.

"So? How was it?"

"Fine."

"That's it? Just fine?"

"Just fine."

"Can I get you something to eat?"

Samuel shook his head. "I've got homework to do."

"You sure? I can—"

"Sorry, Dad." Samuel closed the door.

* * *

Lisa had a little more luck over dinner.

"It's okay," Samuel said, "Might take some getting used to."

"In what way, honey?"

Samuel pushed macaroni cheese around his plate. "I dunno. Just different."

"What are the teachers like?"

"Just teachers."

"What about the other kids," Peter asked. "How's that one who took you to class … Fullerton?"

Samuel stopped chewing. He stared at his plate for a while, then took a sip of water. "He's okay."

"Well you're a real mine of information," Lisa said.

Samuel shrugged again and smiled. "Sorry. There was this big ceremony in the afternoon but I can't tell you anything about it. They swore us all to secrecy." There was the hint of a smile on Samuel's face, so small Peter wondered if he was imagining it.

* * *

Lisa looked up from her laptop. "He's got a bruise."

"What bruise?"

"Christ, Peter, you really are blind sometimes. On his arm. Thought it was weird, him putting on that sweatshirt. I went and had a look once he fell asleep."

Peter was already out of his chair. "I'll go wake him up."

"Sit down you egg."

"It's only his first day at the school. If someone's laid their hands on him I'll—"

"You'll do nothing. Not yet. Leave it until he's ready to talk. Otherwise he'll clam up and never say a thing."

"How do you know?"

"Because that's what you do."

Peter flipped through the channels but there was nothing on.

"I could talk to Bridwell tomorrow."

"What are you going to tell him? Your son's got a bruise you haven't seen and he won't tell you about? He's a good kid, Peter. He'll talk to you. Just give him a few days to get used to things, huh?"

"Yeah, but—" Peter found himself stifling a yawn.

"Look at you. Just as worn out as Samuel. Go get some sleep."

"But the bruise…"

"Will still be there in the morning. Worry then. Sleep now."

Peter let himself be bundled off to bed. He turned off the light and stared out at the darkness.

* * *

Peter woke feeling like he hadn't slept at all, but that couldn't be true. The dream was proof of that. He lay in the darkness, trying to grab on to whatever was left, but he could only summon a single image: a long plain of cracked earth. He was alone under a purpling sky. Though it was cold, the stars rippled as if viewed through a heat haze. The plain was absolutely barren – no trees, or even rocks – just that earth, cracked as if it hadn't seen rain for years. And although the plain was empty, Peter knew there was something just beyond the horizon. He knew what it was, he realised. Or at least, in the frustrating way of dream-logic, he remembered having known what it was. But even that thought was fading now. He felt a weight on his chest and for a second he struggled to breathe.

Then the dream and the suffocating feeling were gone.

He swung his legs over the side of the bed and took a few more deep breaths. The air felt stale in his lungs. In the last few weeks of Melanie's illness, he'd woken like this every morning: terrified, struggling to breathe as if he were drowning. But he hadn't experienced any since she died, until today. He pulled himself to his feet and went to make breakfast.

* * *

Being up early had its advantages. Someone from the school had done a pretty good job of stocking the fridge and pantry. Peter found eggs, bacon, wholemeal toast and some expensive-looking coffee. By the time Samuel wandered downstairs, already dressed, but still rubbing his eyes, Peter had put together a feast.

"What's this?"

"Breakfast."

"Expecting a rugby team to drop in?"

"Aunty Lisa has to go back to Thames today. Thought we should send her off properly."

"She has to go? So soon?"

Lisa emerged from the bathroom, still towelling her hair. "Things to do and people to see, I'm afraid. But I'm not far away. I'll pop back up in a couple of weeks."

Nobody talked while they ate breakfast. Peter had hoped he'd be able to catch a glimpse of the bruise, but he couldn't see anything through Samuel's long-sleeved shirt. Samuel ate quickly and walked away from the table before Peter was halfway through his coffee.

"What's the hurry?"

"Thought I might walk to school this morning. I want to get out the door early."

"Really?" Peter put down his cup. "Aunty Lisa's bus doesn't go until eleven. There's plenty of time for me to run you to school."

Samuel shook his head. "Nah. It's okay. I just want to walk."

Peter shrugged. "Suit yourself."

"What do you think?" he asked after Samuel headed back upstairs. "Think he's trying to keep me from asking about the bruise?"

"Maybe. But maybe not. Perhaps he really does just want to walk. Get a feel for the neighbourhood."

"Maybe."

Lisa stifled a yawn.

"You'll be pretty happy to get back to your own bed," Peter said.

"No, I was right. Your couch is actually really comfortable. But I kept waking up. Weird dreams."

"How do you mean weird?"

"You know, just weird."

"You're as informative as Samuel." Peter grabbed the empty dishes from the table and carried them to the sink.

"It was like I was lost. In some kind of desert?"

The plates slipped from Peter's grip. Most of them landed noisily in the sink, but one smashed on the floor. Peter stood, barefoot, amidst sharp shards.

"Ah, you egg. Look what you've done. Don't move." Lisa went to fetch the broom.

* * *

There was no sign of a bus when they arrived. He walked Lisa to the stop but they were the only people there. "Sure there's a bus coming?"

"We're just early. You were in too much of a hurry to get me out of the house."

"That's not—" he started to say, but Lisa held up a hand.

"I'm only yanking your chain. I know it's going to be weird. Call me any time you need, okay?"

"I'll wait with you."

"Unnecessary, little brother." She pointed to the departures sign. "Thirty minutes. I can look after myself for thirty minutes. Anyway, looks like I'm not the only one who turned up early."

A black Saab stopped on the other side of the road and a man in a suit climbed out of the passenger side. He didn't have any luggage. He crossed the street, checked the departures sign and stood next to the bus stop.

"You're sure?"

Lisa snorted. "Dude. I'm a grown-ass woman."

"Call me when you get back to Thames?"

"It'll be the first thing I do. Now go do something important, you fancy Aucklander."

Just before he turned onto Manukau Road Peter took another look in the rear-view mirror. Lisa had her head down, looking at her phone. The man was reading a newspaper. Peter pulled out into the traffic.

* * *

He told himself he wasn't waiting near the door just so he could get a glimpse of Samuel when he got in. But it was nearly three-thirty and there he was, sitting at the kitchen table where he had a good view of the living room and the front door beyond. When he heard footsteps on the path outside he put down his coffee cup.

Samuel came in quietly, almost bent over. His hair hung in front of his face.

"Hey, buddy," Peter said, hoping the fear he felt didn't carry in his voice. "How was your day? Can I get you something to drink?"

Samuel shook his head.

"Everything okay?"

Samuel looked up. The bruise ran from his cheekbone to the corner of his eye. "I told you Dad," Samuel said, "Everything is fine."

Peter took a step back. "Who did this to you?"

Samuel didn't speak.

"You need to tell me, Samuel. I need to make sure Principal Bridwell is aware that—"

"I can handle it."

"Samuel, this isn't something *you* need to handle. I'll call Principal Bridwell now."

"You won't tell anyone," Samuel's voice was so soft it was almost a whisper. But there was a strength behind it that made Peter look at his son again. The bruise stood out stark and angry on his cheek. But Samuel's face was expressionless.

"Samuel, it's not fair, I'm your father," Peter could hear the whining in his voice and he hated himself for it. He fell silent.

Samuel stared at Peter, waiting to see if he was going to say anything more. Peter lowered his head. He felt like he'd just lost an important battle.

Samuel turned away. "I've got homework."

* * *

Samuel didn't emerge from his room for the rest of the evening. Peter sat downstairs, flicking through channels on the TV, but not settling on anything for more than a couple of minutes. Several times he found himself standing, walking halfway to the stairs, but forced himself to sit back down. He wanted more than anything to talk to Samuel, but he still felt sore from the conversation earlier, as if he were the one with the bruise, not Samuel. He paced, did the dishes, then a load of laundry.

Lisa didn't call, which didn't surprise Peter at all. She would have had every intention of letting him know she'd arrived safely for about five minutes after getting on the bus. Then she would have found some interesting gossip on her phone and forgotten completely. He picked up his phone a few times, and then put it back on the coffee table. He knew what she'd say if he told her about the new bruise. She'd tell him to get on the phone to Bridwell right away and let him know. Then she'd be up all night worrying too.

So he sat. He felt a pressure building around the sides of his skull. He closed his eyes and took a few deep breaths. After Melanie's diagnosis he'd started suffering from panic attacks, and they always started like this. Then he'd get agitated and have trouble breathing. He'd tried to hide them from Melanie. After all, what was a little freak-out compared to what she was going through? But she was too smart for that. *It's okay*, she'd say, as if she hadn't been chugging painkillers all day. *Just let it out. Close your eyes. Breathe.*

So he sat and he closed his eyes and he breathed. Eventually he felt the pressure easing. He leaned back on the couch and looked up at the ceiling. His head felt clearer, as if he'd been for a walk around the block.

He went upstairs. Samuel's door was closed. He knocked and when there was no response he quietly opened the door. Samuel was already in bed. New textbooks were stacked up on his desk. It annoyed him that Samuel hadn't bothered to say goodnight. Samuel looked younger when he was asleep and Peter felt a pang of loss. How many times had they stood just like this, him and Melanie, looking down at their boy's face? Back when the future was as open and unmarked as Samuel's new exercise books.

It had to be Fullerton. Peter thought about the look the boy had given him in Bridwell's office. A rich kid with attendance at Saint Enoch's as a birthright – the little psychopath had probably tormented Samuel and didn't even think about it afterwards. He'd go in to school tomorrow. Bridwell would be shocked to hear that Samuel was being bullied, especially in his first week. He'd sort it out. It would feel good to call Lisa, let her know he'd sorted everything.

Peter closed Samuel's door.

* * *

He was walking barefoot on the plain of cracked earth. The sky was not quite the same as it had been in his last dream. The purple hue was darker now. The air had a sharp, acidic taste, something like iron. He wondered about the dust he was kicking up with every step. Perhaps it would be wise to stop walking, let the dust settle.

Something was over the horizon. Then he felt a twist, as if his mind had seen what was there, then quickly turned away, as if it was trying to protect him from something he should not see.

But he had to see.

He willed himself to move forward. A breeze picked up and he coughed against the dust. He hadn't gone more than fifty paces before the wind became a sandstorm. He closed his eyes but he could feel the sand rasping against his skin. More than anything he wanted to stop, turn around, and run the other way. He knew with the certainty of dream logic that if he did the storm would cease, but he lowered his head and took another step, then another.

The wind screamed in his ears and stole the air from his mouth.

* * *

Bridwell was in a meeting so the receptionist asked Peter to wait. He took a seat on a couch next to a cabinet full of trophies. The walls were covered with framed pictures of past students in poses of triumph: a film director receiving an Oscar; the captain of the Auckland Blues hoisting the Ranfurly shield; a faded newspaper article from the eighties featuring a bespectacled man in a suit under the headline 'The Ten Million Dollar Man'.

Prominently placed off to one side, the award-winning photo of the current Prime Minister from last year's profile in *The Guardian*. Barefoot in the wet sand of Bethells Beach in winter, hands thrust into the pockets of his expensive jeans, smiling at something behind the photographer. Paul couldn't stand the guy, had never voted for him, but he'd read the article. It was little more than a puff piece but he could understand how his party had swept into power in a landslide two years ago. In the article the Prime Minister had spoken of his time at St. Enoch's in glowing terms. There had always been a small number of boarding students and the now-Prime Minister had been one of them when his parents were killed. They had been returning to their home in Napier after a day trip to the beach at Waimarama. The 1958 Bedford truck was unregistered, with three bald tyres. The driver was well past eighty and had not held a driver's license for two years when his left arm went numb, his chest began to burn, and the truck drifted over the centre line. "I wouldn't be here today," the Prime Minister had said in the profile, "and I certainly would not have become Prime Minister without the drive and persistence I was taught in five glorious years at St. Enoch's." That sentence had probably resulted in a 20% increase in fees the next year.

Peter noticed his leg was jiggling up and down. He stopped it and took a few deep breaths. He heard Melanie's voice in his head again. Just let it out. Close your eyes. Breathe.

"Mr Wilson?"

Peter opened his eyes.

"You can go in now," the receptionist said.

Bridwell came out from behind his desk. "Mr Wilson, so good to see you again. Please, take a seat." There were a couple of chairs and a low table in the corner of the office. "Would you like a coffee?"

Peter shook his head. "No, I'm fine."

"How is Samuel adjusting to life at St. Enoch's?"

"He's ... well, there's a problem. He's—" Peter had been running this discussion over in his mind all morning, but here he was and he couldn't get the words out. "He's ... I think he's being bullied."

Bridwell's looked dismayed. "Oh my, and this is still only his first week."

"Well, yes. It's—"

"What makes you think he's being bullied?"

"He comes home and goes straight to his room. I've barely seen him the last couple of days."

Bridwell nodded. "The first few days at a new school can be tough, particularly when you're adapting to a new city as well. He's probably overwhelmed with everything. Perhaps he's just exhausted when he gets home."

"He's got a black eye."

Bridwell didn't say anything for several seconds. "Oh dear," he said. "You must be feeling terrible."

"It doesn't matter how I feel. Someone is hitting my son!" Peter could feel his face flushing red. He hadn't meant to raise his voice.

"As I'm sure you know, we take a zero-tolerance approach to bullying at St. Enoch's. If someone has been bullying your son, you have my word I will find out."

"Wait – what do you mean *if?*"

"You say he has a black eye, but we don't know what happened. I'll talk to his teachers and some of the prefects and try to get to the bottom of what happened." Bridwell smiled, obviously an attempt to calm the father down, but the sight of it just made Peter angry.

"But he's being bullied! It's that prefect who took him to class yesterday."

Bridwell frowned. "That's a serious accusation to make, Mr Wilson. What makes you think Fullerton might be harming your son?"

Peter started to reply. Closed his mouth.

Bridwell smiled softly. "I'll find out what's been happening and let you know. I'll be in touch. Don't worry, Mr Wilson. I've been a Principal for many years. I've found that these things have a way of working themselves out."

He was obviously being dismissed. Peter wanted to say something, to let Bridwell know what he really thought of his precious St. Enoch's, but instead he found himself on his feet, walking towards the door.

"Oh, Mr Wilson."

Peter turned.

"I do hope we'll see you at the mixer this Friday night. It's a chance for you to see a different side to the school. I think you might really appreciate it."

Peter found himself smiling, hated himself for it. "I'll see you there."

* * *

The house felt like a prison when he returned home. He'd already made the beds and tidied the place before his meeting with Bridwell, so there was nothing to do. It was going to be a scorcher of a day. He should make the most of being an Aucklander now – do some exploring, visit the shops, go to the beach, but he was shattered. Those bloody dreams had ruined his sleep for the whole week. They hung around during the day too. Several times he'd closed his eyes just for a couple of seconds and found himself back there, walking barefoot on that cracked plain under those glistening stars. He blinked. Had he nodded off standing in the kitchen? For a second he thought about taking himself back to bed, but he had never slept well during the day, and he didn't think today was going to be any different. He put a couple of spoons of instant coffee in a cup. Then he added a couple more.

He called Lisa again while he waited for the kettle, but there was still no answer. He left her another message. His voice echoed in the empty kitchen.

He looked up at the ceiling. Samuel's room was directly above the kitchen.

He stood in the doorway, holding an empty plastic bag. *I'm not spying*, he told himself. *I'm tidying*.

Samuel's room was spotless. He'd made his bed, just as he'd done the last two days. The first couple of times Peter had been impressed – Samuel had never been so tidy at home, but something about the perfectly turned-down duvet, completely free of wrinkles, felt wrong.

He crouched down and peered under the bed. Normally he'd expect to see half-finished muesli bars and potato chip wrappers, along with several weeks' worth of laundry, but it was spotless.

Peter opened the top drawer of the dresser. Socks on the left, underwear on the right, perfectly organised. The next drawer was full of t-shirts, perfectly folded. Samuel was just a kid. Kids were supposed to be messy and smelly and complain about cleaning their room. They didn't turn into neat freaks overnight. It just didn't happen.

There was something balled up at the very back of the bottom drawer. Peter had to stare at it for several seconds before he could understand what he was seeing – one of Samuel's new white uniform shirts. Whatever had happened to the thing, Samuel couldn't have been wearing it at the time. One of the arms had been ripped off completely. The arm that was still attached was shredded with long, straight cuts that ran from shoulder to cuff. And on the front was a bloodstain larger than his fist.

He dropped the shirt. It lay on the floor in the middle of the bedroom like something dragged from the sea. After a while he picked it up again and shoved it back in the bottom drawer where he'd found it.

* * *

The afternoon passed with nothing to show for it. He wanted, needed, to talk to Samuel about the shirt, but he couldn't see how. If he mentioned it, Samuel would know Peter had been in his room, but it wasn't as if he could say nothing. He couldn't stop thinking about it. Peter had always been a confident parent, from the moment he'd first heard Samuel's newborn cry. At every phase in their life together he'd somehow known exactly what to do, what to say. Even at the worst of times, the last few weeks of Melanie's life and the desolate months that followed, his relationship with Samuel had always been there. They still had each other, and he'd thought they always would. He suddenly felt like he was living with a stranger.

Samuel didn't arrive home until nearly five. Peter jumped up from the table when he heard the door rattle and nearly ran across the kitchen. He forced himself to slow down a little, then stopped dead when he saw.

"What happened?"

Samuel's sleeves were rolled up. He raised his right hand. His knuckles were raw. Samuel clenched his fist and fresh blood began to flow, ran down his forearm to his elbow. Dripped on the floor. Samuel looked at his own blood as if it were an exotic insect he was seeing for the first time.

"I told you not to go to Bridwell. I told you I could handle it." A slow smile spread across Samuel's face, turned into a sneer. "It's been handled."

A buzzing started in Peter's head. He took a step backwards, felt his back hit the wall.

"I need a shower," Samuel said. "And then I have homework." He looked down at the blood fallen from his fist, a stain now spreading across the carpet. "Clean that up."

Peter closed his eyes for a moment. When he looked again Samuel was gone. Samuel didn't leave his room for the rest of the night and when Peter woke the next morning he found himself alone.

* * *

He'd been telling himself a story the whole afternoon. Samuel would come home and say he didn't want to go. They'd go out to dinner instead, check out a movie. They'd gorge themselves on ice cream and popcorn, stay up too late and sleep in the next day. It would be the perfect evening, just the two of them. But Samuel came home and went straight to his room, without a word.

Peter waited as long as he could. Then he went upstairs and knocked on Samuel's door. "Hey, buddy? You still keen on going to this thing tonight? We could skive off and go see a movie instead. You know … if you wanted?"

Samuel opened the door, but only a crack. "No. We're going."

"Oh. Okay. Well, I was just wondering—"

The door closed again.

Peter's suit was still hanging on the back of the door, right where he'd left it. He'd taken it off as soon as he got back from dropping Samuel off at the school on Monday. Wearing a suit twice in a week. The last time before that had been Melanie's funeral.

He tried to call Lisa a couple more times. When her recorded voice asked him to leave a message he hung up. He'd already left enough.

Samuel appeared in the living room just before seven. He was wearing his uniform, tie straight, shoes polished.

"Looking sharp son," Peter said. Samuel shrugged.

Samuel didn't say a word the whole drive. Peter kept wanting to say something, anything, to break the silence, but he kept quiet as well. There had been a Saint Enoch's monastery once, back before the school. Peter didn't know if the monks were the kind that took a vow of silence. Perhaps that had something to do with the way all the conversations he tried to start with people from Saint Enoch's sputtered and died. Even with his own son.

He gripped the steering wheel and looked out into the night.

* * *

Peter hadn't been in the school hall before. Even if he had, he might not have recognised it. Thick red curtains hung from the ceiling, hiding all the gym equipment. Jazz played through the PA speakers. If it were not for the lines of the basketball court still visible on the floor, Peter could have sworn he was at a yacht club.

It was crowded. All the men wore expensive suits. The women wore thin, silky dresses. Peter pulled at the collar of his shirt again. His suit hung awkwardly on him, as if he'd recently gained weight, or lost it.

Bridwell was waiting near the door. "Mr Wilson. So glad you could make it. Good evening, Samuel."

"Good evening Alastair," Samuel said, and the familiarity in Samuel's voice was like a dagger in Peter's back.

Someone called from across the room. A group of kids were leaning against the wall. Samuel walked over to join them.

"Could I offer you a drink?"

"Thank you, yes." *God, yes.*

A table near the door was covered with plates of canapés and bottles of wine. Bridwell poured two glasses, handed one to Peter and raised his own in a toast. "To new beginnings."

The wine was really very good, and strong. Peter's head began to spin after a couple of sips.

Fullerton pulled himself away from the wall and wrapped his arms around Samuel's shoulders. Peter expected Samuel to flinch, but he leaned into the hug and pounded Fullerton on the back as if they'd been best friends for years.

Fullerton said something and all the boys, including Samuel, burst out laughing. Peter wondered if he'd been wrong about the older boy. And if he'd been wrong about Fullerton, perhaps he'd been wrong about everything. The image of Samuel's torn and bloodied shirt rose again in his mind, but it suddenly seemed far away and unimportant.

Peter raised his glass again. "To St. Enoch's."

The wine was really very good.

* * *

Bridwell walked him around the room and made introductions. Peter smiled but wasn't capable of much more. It might have been the hum of conversation, but Peter struggled to make out the names and professions Bridwell rattled off. This one was a newscaster. That one had just retired from a twenty-year political career. There were lawyers, doctors, and members of the boards of the largest companies on the New Zealand Stock Exchange. Bridwell just kept moving him from one handshake to another. The smiles didn't reach their eyes. There was an excess of teeth. And suddenly Peter's head felt far too heavy. He took a step back, stumbled, fell against the wall.

"Are you okay?"

Peter blinked. Bridwell was leaning over him, a concerned expression on his face.

"I'm ... Yeah. Fine. Just tired. Good wine." He looked at his glass and was surprised to see it was already empty.

Bridwell nodded. "I haven't given you the grand tour yet, have I?"

Peter shook his head.

"Come on then," Bridwell said. "A walk might clear your

head a little."

He looked back as they left the gym. Samuel was still laughing with his friends.

The cold air hit him as soon as they were out the door.

Bridwell set out towards the playing fields at a brisk pace. Peter walked faster, struggling to keep up. When he reached the middle of the field, Bridwell stopped. "Beautiful, aren't they? There's so much light pollution in Auckland, but out here you can still see a few. I'm sure you're used to a far less polluted sky out in the country."

Peter looked up. There was a halo of light from houses on the other side of the fields, but if he looked straight up he could see a few stars: the Southern Cross, Orion's belt.

"It's funny," Peter said. "I never really thought to look up."

Bridwell nodded. "We get so tied up in the minutiae of life. I'm the same. Whenever I'm working late I come out here before I head home. To remind myself what's really important."

"The stars?"

Bridwell smiled. "What about you, Mr Wilson? What's the most important thing in your life?"

Peter didn't have to think about it. "Samuel. There's nothing else now. I'd do anything for him." Peter was surprised to hear the words tumble out of him, even though they were true. The fog might have faded from his head, but he was obviously still feeling the effects of the wine.

"I understand. I feel the same way about the students."

The school chapel was on the other side of the playing fields.

"The chapel is older than the school," Bridwell said. "In fact, it's even older than the monastery that was here before the school. It was built in 1865. Back then it would have been the only stone building for miles. The stars must have been spectacular."

Bridwell produced a key from his pocket and placed it in an ancient lock. The door opened with a creak. "Sorry," he said. "I keep meaning to ask one of the caretakers to oil that. A five-minute job, but I never seem to remember. Something more important always crops up."

They stepped through the door into darkness.

Bridwell flicked on a torch. Peter couldn't see much of the interior, just the backs of wooden pews and the shadow of an altar at the front. Bridwell waved the torch towards the wall. Hidden in a small alcove were steps leading down. "Be careful here," Bridwell said. "Bit of a Health and Safety nightmare, I'm afraid."

Bridwell started down and Peter followed. He couldn't see anything apart from Bridwell's back and the tiniest of lights from the torch. The air grew colder. There was a damp smell that reminded him of iron.

"Ah. Here we are."

Peter felt the last stair. He stepped down onto rough, uneven rock. They seemed to be in a cave.

Bridwell turned off the torch.

"Good one," Peter said. "Could you turn the light on again before I trip and break my neck?"

He couldn't hear Bridwell at all. He waited, concentrating on the dark, but the only sound was his own breathing.

"Fine," Peter said. "If you're going to be a dick, I'll see you outside." He turned around, stretching out his foot for the step, but he stumbled against the wall.

He had to be close to the stairs. He reached into his pocket for his phone. The screen was so bright it nearly blinded him.

He winced and waved the phone across the wall, but it only showed what some deep part of him already knew. There was no staircase.

He followed the line of the wall, looking for an explanation. His fingers found the answer before the light did: a metal door, flush with the surrounding rock. So Bridwell had led him down here, then silently backed away and closed the door. "Missed your calling," Peter muttered. "You should have been a comedian."

He refused to panic. He wasn't going to give Bridwell the satisfaction of a freak-out. "You private school people are all the same," he muttered. "Just a bunch of wankers."

He took a few steps away from the wall. It was a big space. The light from his phone screen didn't reach the ceiling.

He was surprised to find his phone still had a signal. There weren't many numbers on it. He selected Lisa and hit dial. His phone beeped and connected. Something buzzed on the other side of the room and Peter saw a light. Bridwell pulled a phone from his pocket, stared at the screen for a moment, then hit a button. Peter's phone disconnected.

"You would have been proud of her," Bridwell said. "She put up a good fight. She screamed when Luther dragged her to the car. If there had been anyone else around, or if the bus hadn't been late, she might have made things complicated for us."

"Where is she?" Peter couldn't hide the tremor in his voice.

Bridwell dropped Lisa's phone on the floor. The screen went black as it crunched under his heel. "It doesn't matter," he said.

A hand grabbed Peter's wrist and his phone slipped from his grip. The screen flashed once as it clattered across the floor, and in that instant he saw the others surrounding him.

"You can scream too, if you want." The voice in his ear was

barely a whisper, but Peter recognised it. Fullerton. He struggled uselessly. The boy was stronger than he looked.

"The chosen see visions sometimes," Bridwell said. "Tell me, Mr Wilson, have you experienced any strange dreams lately?"

There was light now, just a little. Two students stepped towards him, each holding a small candle. They looked like altar boys, except they weren't in white vestments. They wore heavy robes, deep red, except where age had faded them to a pallid grey.

"I know we seem like – what did you call us? A bunch of wankers, but we're proud of our ways. They burn in us, just as they did in our Founder."

"What the hell are you talking about? Saint Enoch was the mother of Saint Kentigern, the daughter of a Scottish king."

"I didn't know you were a student of religion."

"I Googled it."

"Ah. Well. It's a common misapprehension. Our school is named for Enoch Bowen, the greatest of all saints, though not a Catholic one. A great man, and an endless source of wisdom. He gives us so much and asks for so little in return."

He heard shuffling. Something brushed against the back of his legs. People were on their hands and knees behind him. Fullerton and another boy pushed him gently backwards until he was lying across the backs of children.

"Don't feel too bad, Mister Wilson. It's not your fault. What with your wife's unfortunate situation, no close friends, no family except a sister who won't be missed, there was nothing you could do. You were a sparrow in a hurricane from the moment we delivered the letter."

Another robed figure emerged from the darkness.

It was Samuel.

"You don't need to worry. I will look after your son," Bridwell said. "I've never seen a child adapt so quickly. There's no telling what he'll accomplish when he leaves school armed with everything he'll learn from us. From *them*."

Something moved just beyond the circle of light. At first Peter thought it was Bridwell, but the shape was too tall and thin, a shadow without a man to cast it, darker than its surroundings. He turned his head and even in the absence of light he could see several more shadows. They loomed over the children like expectant parents.

Samuel held a long dagger with a curved blade. Peter searched Samuel's face and found no trace of the boy he'd been a week ago. He thought again of the shirt he'd found in Samuel's room. It had been Samuel's shirt. Had it been Lisa's blood?

Samuel climbed on top of Peter, the boy's knees digging into Peter's chest. He struggled to breathe.

Samuel raised the dagger above his head.

When the blade caught the candlelight, it shone like a star.

THE GLASSBLOWER'S PEACE
JAMES ROWLAND

Tomaso da Guda chose to remember only one thing about his father: he had too many sons. The proper number was three. With three able-bodied men, a man could plant his seed into the most important areas of Venetian life. The eldest would be trained to go into government. The next would receive some patronage from a rich merchant and be given a berth on his most profitable ship. The youngest would be given to the clergy; it was important to have a direct route into Heaven. Tomaso da Guda knew all this because his father told him these simple truths on his deathbed. Tomaso was his fourth son. He was left to float rudderless through the canals of the city.

From this inheritance, Tomaso chose the most strictly regulated routine he could think of: the army. No-one pointed out to him that in times of perpetual peace, the army wasn't particularly well drilled. Being a soldier mostly meant spending your afternoons moving from bar to bar, trading illusions and downing alcohol to fuel the next round of more outrageous stories. Tomaso didn't care much for the storytelling, instead choosing the quiet, dark corners that existed in every establishment. Still, he was paid well for his drinking. It gave him a modest house and the potential to spin modesty into respectability.

At the very least, he was doing better than his older brothers. The eldest had disappeared into the bowels of some prison after seeking to ban the use of magic within the city's borders. The youngest had drowned. Even in a city like Venice, priests never learned to swim. The deepest cut was his second brother vanishing somewhere north of Egypt, along with the rest of his crew mates. As children, the two of them had banded together against the world and ran through so many cobblestoned streets that they went through shoes twice as fast as anyone else. Now Tomaso was alone, his parents dead, his brothers gone. There was no aunt or uncle to offer an understanding nod and laugh through tales of family joy, no cousin to lend a sympathetic ear. There was no-one. In a way, his father was right. He had too many sons and the spare was left to soldier on alone.

Some days, Tomaso resisted the seductive song of the canals and their many bars. He sat in the barracks and pretended he was doing something important. Often, those days aligned with when the thunderstorms came to Venice, pelting the city with rain and causing the waterways to swell and bulge like a corpse. Tomaso sat alone in the dining room, playing cards spread across the table in the shape of a clock. The other grunts had braved the storm, commandeering boats to take them to the doors of their favourite haunts. Tomaso, though, enjoyed the simple comforts of being warm and dry.

"Private da Guda," a voice said from behind him. Tomaso sent the playing card in his hand flying. "Good to know that there's someone still ready to work."

Turning in his seat, Tomaso squeaked like a mouse and jumped to his feet. His knees banged against the underside of the table and his teeth sunk deep into his lip. General di Barso towered in front of him. His face was grim and slightly pale. The General's moustache was a topic of much discussion in the barracks, the bristles so independently well-behaved. When he walked the cobbled streets of Venice, men and women flocked to kiss his boots. He might as well have been the Pope. He was the face of the Glassblower's Peace, even if the baker down the street had made just as much contribution to it as he had.

"Private," the General said, his moustache perfectly still. "Can you make your way to the Ghetto, and quickly?"

Tomaso stood there, his mind tracing the route out. He could. However, the other privates had taken all the boats. He'd have to trudge through the water-logged streets, walking from one side of Venice to the other, hoping to navigate what was flooding and what were actual canals. Trying to think of a way to tell the General as much without dropping the other soldiers in it, even if they were nothing more than strangers to him, Tomaso was surprised to hear his own voice break the building silence. "Yes, sir. Won't be a problem, sir."

"Good. We need you to visit the Glassblower. Tell her that we have a situation. We've received word that the Ottomans are using this storm as cover to send a fleet. We need it taken care of."

"Uh, sir." Tomaso stared at the General, who was refusing to meet his eyes. "Are we under attack? I mean, if we are, uh, shouldn't someone more senior be taking the message? I can do it, obviously, but, sir, wouldn't it better coming from you?"

"The Glassblower has a difficult relationship with authority. Be an idiot, fawn on her, try not to upset her. And get her to destroy those ships. We can't do anything with this storm over our heads; our fleet would be shredded just trying to leave the lagoon."

Fifteen minutes later, Tomaso was trudging through the water building up over the cobbled streets of Castello. The canals poured into his boots, seeking to colonise his feet. He shivered with every step. The Ghetto was easily half an hour away by foot and already he could feel the wet and cold sinking into his bones. He cursed the other soldiers, the army's boats moored to the front doors of various unsavoury establishments. Misery settled around him like a sea fog. It covered his passage through the city and it was only when the narrow, dark entranceway of the Ghetto appeared in front of him that Tomaso realised the seriousness of his message. Venice was being attacked. For the first time in a century, someone felt they could beat the might of the Venetian navy. Or, more accurately, someone thought they could handle the Glassblower and her magic. The idea seemed ludicrous and that made Tomaso shiver more in the cold. Someone was either mad, powerful, or both.

The Glassblower's home was a lanky building, so skinny it looked as if each floor must have had only one room, and so tall that it still looked as if the building had seven or eight levels. Tomaso knocked on the wooden door. He half expected it to swing open of its own accord. It stayed perfectly still. He knocked again. There was still no response. For a second more he waited and then Tomaso decided that the fate of the city was more important than decorum. He hammered at the wood, yelling and shouting, drawing glares from a multitude of nearby windows until he realised that the door was unlocked. With the turn of a handle and the gentlest of pushes, it swung open to reveal a single, darkened room. Chest puffing and red-faced,

Tomaso stepped inside.

The sound of wind chimes filled the air. Glass clinked together. A melody formed in Tomaso's ears long before his eyes adjusted to the darkness. The tune made him think of harsh Egyptian summer, the air dry and stale on his tongue. The sun hammered down at him, seeking every patch of bare skin, whipping it until it was an angry red welt and then salt filled his mouth, lodging deep into his throat. He was so lost in the music that he didn't spot the wizened old woman until he could have reached out and touched her lined face. Her wispy white hair sat perfectly still atop her head, like a well-behaved cat, and whiskers were beginning to grow out from under her nose. Everything about her, from her posture to her leathery skin, suggested that the weight of an elephant was bearing down on her shoulders from a life well lived. Yet, Tomaso noticed as the music slipped away like water cupped within his hands, her eyes sparkled, two untouched emeralds within her face.

"What did you hear?" the old woman said, walking past him to close the door. "The chimes, I mean. What song did they sing for you?"

"Egypt. The desert. The sun. Water, I think." The truth came tumbling free from Tomaso's mouth before his brain could even begin to concoct a lie. The woman nodded, as if this cleared up some Biblical mystery, and locked the door.

"I'm sorry they didn't bring better news, but people say that truth is preferable. I don't know if I believe that. Now, who sent you? Or are you here in a personal capacity? I don't do commissions anymore. Not enough magic in these old bones and I can't blow glass like I used to. Get all these imperfections these days. Bubbles. Cracks. Can't do anything with that type of glass."

"No, no, ma'am," Tomaso said. "I'm here on behalf of General di Barso."

The Glassblower nodded. "And what does the General want?"

"We're under attack, ma'am. The Ottomans. They're using the storm. Or they caused the storm. We can't send our ships. And they're coming. A whole fleet. They wanted you to do something."

"Well, I see they sent someone who could impart the urgency of the situation," the old woman said with a smirk, and Tomaso realised he was panting. "Just a fleet, is it?" Tomaso nodded. "I suppose they think they'll just have a little raid. Test how I'm doing, make sure I haven't died, and maybe steal a few bits and pieces all at the same time. Very insolent. Take your boots off, I don't want you traipsing water everywhere."

The Glassblower waited until Tomaso had removed one boot before she headed to the stairs. By the time he had removed the second, making sure not to empty too much water over the floor, the old woman was already out of sight. Squelching with every step, Tomaso raced to the stairwell, taking the steps three at a time. A thought was only just sinking into his brain. He was going to see the Glassblower at work. It was a privilege that only a handful of people could say they had witnessed. His palms were wet and it had nothing to do with the rain. The Glassblower was waiting for him on the fourth floor, her hunched frame standing by the door.

"Please don't touch too much, don't want you losing too many limbs." The Glassblower smiled and then stepped through the door.

Following the old woman into the room, Tomaso gasped as he caught sight of the ceiling. It looked as if someone had deconstructed the idea of a chandelier. Hanging down from the various beams, beads of glass swayed in the breeze from one corner of the room to another. There were at least a hundred clear raindrops suspended from the roof. Candlelight glistened off the glass, the room twinkling like a star. It took Tomaso a moment to even realise that he stood in front of a pool, a wide bowl filling out the fourth floor except for a tall, narrow cupboard nestled in the corner. The water rippled along and, if he squinted, Tomaso thought he could see the outline of the long foot of Europe. A gentle throbbing sat where Venice would have been.

"Now, let's see where those ships are," the Glassblower said. She walked to the cupboard and reached inside. Tomaso craned his neck and spied a dozen miniature glass boats, perfectly crafted galleons, within her leathery hand. She released them into the pool with a whisper, the ships riding the water independently of any breeze within the room. The glass flotilla floated closer and closer to the city, hugging the coastline of the Venetian-controlled ports to the east.

"How brazen of them. I didn't know they had the nerve!" the old woman said, shaking her head. Grabbing hold of one of the wooden columns that made up the wall, she pulled and it came away in her hands. A flicker of recognition ran through Tomaso's mind; the column was a ladder. He had seen similar designs before in the majestic governmental library. Letting the ladder run along railings that Tomaso hadn't noticed before, the old woman moved the vertical steps until they were sloping over the pool itself. She wiggled it around, pausing to check the position of the boats before readjusting the ladder. "I'm not much for climbing these days. Could you head up for me, dear?"

Tomaso climbed onto the first step of the ladder before he

even considered the risk of falling into the pool. The Glassblower had asked him to do something and it seemed impossible that he wouldn't. The wood was steady beneath his fingers and any fear of slipping under the water disappeared. Shimmying his way up the ladder, he noticed that a handful of the glass beads hanging from the ceiling were now pulsing a soft red, as if dying embers had slipped inside the raindrops.

"Steady on your feet. That's good. Now just cut those beads from the roof. Only the ones which are glowing, mind you."

Tomaso reached up to take hold of the thread keeping the glass secure, testing its strength against his skin. Opening his mouth, ready to ask how he was meant to cut the fabric, he felt the thread snap between his fingers. The glass beads fell from the ceiling. The first raindrop collided against one of the ships, shattering the vessel into a hundred pieces, all of them instantly slipping beneath the surface of the pool. The next three beads crashed into the water. A colossal wave rolled out, sucking in another two ships, dragging them into the churning sea. In several seconds, the entire miniature fleet was destroyed, its remains floating harmlessly out into the Mediterranean.

"That should be that then," the Glassblower said. "Now will you stay for some tea?"

Tomaso spluttered, chewing on his bottom lip. Had they actually done anything? Staring at the pool, he watched the few remaining shards of glass float further away from the city. Had something happened to the real Ottoman fleet? A shiver ran through his spine at the thought of returning to the barracks and telling the General he had stayed for tea while the fleet drew closer.

"Is the fleet gone?" he asked, and the old woman nodded.

"I should be going. Should tell the General." The Glassblower shrugged and wandered from the room.

Two hours later, his boots now so filled with water that he felt he was carrying the entire Grand Canal between his toes, Tomaso stood in an austere side room with General di Barso. They were staring at a glass box, not much larger than a child's hand. It began to vibrate on the table, a slip of paper escaping from a slot from the top. The General plucked the note before Tomaso could even blink.

"Gone. The entire fleet," General di Barso said. "Nothing left but a few planks of wood and plaintive screams."

It was only then, as he knew that Venice was safe, did Tomaso realise he didn't even ask the Glassblower for her name.

* * *

"Gilulia Seguso," the old woman said, her thinning eyebrows driving up into her forehead. Tomaso wondered when the last time someone had asked her for her name was. "And what is yours?"

"Tomaso da Guda."

"Well, introductions have been made," Gilulia said. Tomaso thought he saw the hint of a smile, the barest upturn at the corner of her mouth. "Now explain to me again what is happening."

Upon his arrival at Gilulia's home, the old woman had led him up the winding staircase until she ushered him into the attic. Tomaso had expected all manner of things. Perhaps glass animals wandering through the room, or stacks of miniature cities ready to be crushed if their governments threatened the Glassblower's Peace. Instead, he found himself wandering into a compressed model of a home. In one corner was a tiny kitchen, a mess of copper and brass, while in the other was a small bed. Sat equidistant between them were an old, wooden table and two bulging armchairs. Tomaso was squeezed into one of them a few minutes later, a glass shoved into his hand. Almost word for word, he retold Gilulia what the General had told him. Apparently, he had a "working relationship" with the Glassblower now and as soon as the Ottomans were moving again, Tomaso was sent for.

"What I don't understand is why they're trying again? If they were just testing the peace, I sent them enough of a warning last time," Gilulia said. She stared hard at Tomaso's face before taking a sip of her drink.

"I don't know," Tomaso shrugged. "Is it important? They're coming to burn the city! And the General said their ships have some sort of protective coating."

"Oh, I know all about their shields. A stupid idea. Emir Mehmed is so obsessed in his own brilliance that he never thinks about other people's. A glassblower isn't worried about some carpets. No, that's not the problem, Tomaso. The problem is why they even feel the need to attack. Did that walking medal say anything about that?"

Tomaso paused. The General had said nothing about the politics. Who was he to ask? He was just a private. "No, ma'am," Tomaso said. Gilulia took another sip of her wine, saying nothing. The silence grew longer and he felt its fingernails digging into his soul, scratching at his conscience. "But I can ask for you?" the words tumbling free from his mouth.

"That's very kind of you. Yes, I think that's a good idea. But don't tell them I want to know," Gilulia said. There was a real smile on her face now. "Well, let's not waste any more time. Let's deal with the Emir's glorified haberdashery."

As they worked their way back down the stairs, Tomaso juggled the several vials that were shoved into his arms. Once they were on the bottom floor, Gilulia stepped past the kilns and various instruments, moving away from the front door. Tomaso spotted a door at the back of the room. He hadn't noticed it before. He had learnt the entire house was like that. As long as a person didn't pay attention to every wall, every nook and cranny, there was something that would be left hidden. It left Tomaso constantly checking over his shoulder, waiting for something to lunge out of the darkness. He followed Gilulia quickly to the back door. She opened it and a narrow canal appeared in front of them, waiting to swallow them whole. Right underneath the door, tethered by a wooden peg, was a small gondola. A shiver ran down his spine as he noticed the boat was made entirely from glass. The murky green water stared back at him from under the hull.

"In you get," Gilulia said, stepping aside to let Tomaso climb in.

He paused just long enough for the old woman to tut loudly and then he lowered himself in the boat, almost invisible, trusting entirely on Gilulia that he wasn't about to tumble into the canal. The gondola took his weight easily. Tomaso felt the knot in his stomach untie itself. Putting the vials down by his feet, he reached up and helped Gilulia into the boat. He got the impression that she wanted to swat away his hand and slide into the gondola with all the grace of a dancer, and yet as the boat shifted on the gentle throbbing of the Venetian heartbeat, Tomaso felt her fingers wrap tight around his own, clinging to him as she dropped into the boat. As Gilulia settled into her end of the boat, Tomaso smiled at her and he felt a surge of affection for the old woman, who felt less mythical and more human. Reaching over the side of the boat, Gilulia patted the side of the gondola like a man would to a horse. The boat rocked forward and began to glide through the canal.

"Just remember to stay quiet, Tomaso," Gilulia said. Her eyes were locked on a point just above his right shoulder. "No startled yelps if you please. And not too many questions for now."

Turning, Tomaso looked for what Gilulia had been staring at. His eyes went wide. They had turned into a narrow, side canal, barely wide enough for the gondola to fit through. At the end of it was a pane of glass. A thousand questions whistled through his brain and all of them had been forbidden. The boat continued to pick up speed. They were still moving at just a trickle and yet it felt as if they were hurtling toward the glass. Every muscle within Tomaso's body tensed for the impact, his eyes clamped shut and yet the gondola drove through it without a sound, a tingle passing over his skin as if they slipped under a warm waterfall. When he opened his eyes again, Venice had vanished. The canal and the tall, narrow buildings standing guard on either side had transformed into the ever-stretching sea. The boat was drifting in open water, unperturbed by the wild waves lapping around them. The dark of night was punctured by pinpricks of lights floating on the horizon.

"Now, keep your voice down," Gilulia said, her voice barely beating the roaring of the sea. "They won't see the gondola, and the Mediterranean won't trouble us. But they still might spot us. They'll hopefully see us as driftwood, but driftwood doesn't talk. It doesn't even think."

While he could resist opening his mouth, Tomaso couldn't

turn off his brain. How far had they travelled? Where were they? And what were the lights floating in front of them? The questions swirled through his head as the gondola chased the specks. They grew brighter and brighter and soon, with a little help from the universe above, Tomaso could make out the shape of a dozen ships, the Ottoman flotilla tacking toward Venice. He should have been fearful. His hands should have gone clammy and his bowels twitched. They were drifting toward an Ottoman fleet, a private and an old woman, sitting in a glass gondola. To the untrained eye, they were floating to their doom. Yet Tomaso knew better. There was an utter conviction inside his stomach that he was about to witness the entire destruction of the flotilla.

Gilulia didn't say a word until the gondola was slipping between the two rearmost ships. Now that they were closer, Tomaso could make out the material clinging to the warships. It was carpet. Wound tightly around the vessels, various patterns and symbols sewn into the fabric, the carpet clung to the ships like a protective shield. Tomaso could only stare at something as off-putting as a ship made of rugs. Gilulia paid it no heed. She reached forward and took one of the vials from the floor. She inspected it, running her finger along the glass, nodding. "Take this one and fill it with water."

Doing as he was told, Tomaso pulled the stopper from the vial and dipped the glass under the sea. When he pulled it away, though, the container was filled with a thick, inky black substance instead of salt water. A question bubbled up through his throat before he remembered his orders. He swallowed it back down and waited for the next command.

Gilulia stared at him. "Pour it out then."

Tomaso chewed on his lip, his cheeks prickling with heat. He felt like a fool as he emptied the vial he had just filled back into the sea. Yet, the viscous black puddle sat atop the sea, refusing to be broken down. He sniffed the top of the vial and a repugnant, heavy smell invaded his nostrils. Gilulia ordered him to repeat the task over and over as they drifted between the various ships of the flotilla. Behind them, the inky slickness seeped out, lapping against the carpeted hulls of the Ottoman navy. Tomaso was certain that a sailor would notice them, but even those lookouts up in the rigging didn't seem to spot them or their black shadow behind them. He wasn't sure if they were within the naval nest for fifteen minutes or an hour, but eventually they were drifting out into open waters again.

"That's enough now," Gilulia said, interrupting pours. "Just hold on tight and don't stick anything outside the boat."

She reached down by his feet and pulled another one of the vials up, a ruby embedded in the glass. Her fingers ran down its curves like someone teasing their lover. Rolling up her sleeve, Gilulia plunged her arm beneath the sea. When she pulled it back up, there was fire blazing within the glass. The flame licked up against the edge of the vial. Somewhere behind them, a shout went out from one of the ships. It was too late. Gilulia tapped the edge of the glass and it shattered, the fire falling to the sea. The black substance on the water ignited. Tomaso felt the heat fly at him, suffocating him in its grip. Behind them, the Mediterranean was on fire. Gilulia moved back into the middle of the boat, holding tightly onto her seat. Even with Tomaso's heartbeat racing, it took only several thumps for the entire fleet to go up in flames. The carpets were powerless against the fires and a storm of screams began to blow out from the ships.

"I thought the carpets were meant to protect the ships,"

Tomaso said, the words coming out so quiet that he repeated himself.

"Oh, it would have against most things. But if you can destroy a carpet with fire, then you can destroy a magic carpet with magic fire." Gilulia tapped the side of the glass gondola, the boat picking up speed as it flew back to Venice. As they travelled, the pair talked about stars and glass, families and hurt. They exchanged little parts of themselves, tiny shards of their identity, under the moonlight. The Ottoman fleet was already ash behind them.

* * *

"Private da Guda, why are you still here?" the General said, looking up from his desk. Tomaso couldn't stop his left leg from twitching.

"Why do they keep attacking, sir?"

General di Barso looked back down at his desk, moving papers around. "That's not something a private really needs to know, is it?"

"With respect, sir," Tomaso said, the twitch now spreading to his right leg. "I'm not just a private now. You send me to talk to Gil … the Glassblower. I'm the one who ends up accompanying her on her missions. I've been in the middle of the Ottoman fleets. I've travelled to the Shadow Realm. I've talked with reflections. I think I at least deserve to know why." He did his best to appear indignant. While Tomaso was curious at the extent of the Ottomans' aggression, he really only cared because he had promised Gilulia he would ask. Since he made that promise, he couldn't meet her eyes whenever she asked him if he had

127

questioned the General about the Ottomans' aggression.

"Very well. Though I suggest you don't inflate your sense of worth too highly. Simply put, the Turks are practising a very aggressive form of defence. Some countries are not blessed with stability like ours. And when we spot dynastic squabbles in our enemies, it is our duty, as servants of the Republic, to take advantage of that. There are several profitable ports that we feel are vulnerable. These attacks on us are simply a distraction to keep us from claiming them."

The twitching in Tomaso's legs stopped. Mouth hanging open, even his fingers refused to move. The General's words ran around his skull. They didn't make any sense. The Glassblower's Peace was constant; it never changed. The various polemic articles and history books in their infancy made clear the conditions of the Peace. Gilulia Seguso's magic was like nothing Venice had ever seen before and when the government came to seek the assistance of the young woman, she had named one condition. She was to be a shield and never a sword. Her magic was to protect Venetians, a silent guardian. The Glassblower's Peace was never to become the Glassblower's War and yet here was the General explaining that that was exactly what had happened. The government and army were taking advantage of her. His hands turned to fists.

"You're excused, Private," General di Barso said, his eyebrows raised when he looked up from his desk.

Working his way through the arteries of the city, Tomaso ignored the offer of several boats ready to taxi him somewhere else. Walking felt right. He worked out his anger through his feet. His boots slapped down hard against the street, the stab of pain in his heel a comfort. Every separate cobble was the General's face.

Tomaso couldn't believe Gilulia was being taken advantage of. His stomach churned. He tried to imagine what such a betrayal would taste like. Picturing his father turning to him, revealing that his entire family were imposters, Tomaso felt sick and even then, he knew it would have been a mere slight compared to what had happened to Gilulia. He bit back the desire to vomit into the canal. Gilulia thought she was defending the city, that she was killing its enemies to protect her fellow Venetians. Instead, she had killed men who were just trying to save their own people. Tomaso couldn't imagine such a thing.

An hour later, he was sitting in Gilulia's attic, absent-mindedly chewing a mouthful of fish she had given him for supper. The old woman eased herself into the chair across from him. She frowned. He hadn't touched their long-running game of counters. "Enough moping now, you're putting me on edge. What's wrong?"

"There's an army coming. Ten thousand strong. They're coming to burn Venice."

While walking earlier, Tomaso decided on a course of action. He wouldn't tell Gilulia about the government's deceit. It would only hurt her. In her ignorance, the wound remained closed and unnoticed. Also, the thought slapping him across his face, he would be risking all of Venice's safety. He couldn't rule out her being so offended that she would refuse to help. The army would be left to fight the Ottomans unaided and they would almost certainly lose. The city would burn. No, he wouldn't tell her. Yet, Tomaso looked up at the mirror above the fireplace and saw something twisted and ugly looking back at him. A rough approximation of his face, riddled with pox and scarred beyond all possibilities, stared where his reflection should have been. He imagined the General's reflection would have looked the same.

"It's all a fraud, Gilulia. All of it. The Ottomans aren't attacking us; we're attacking them! Trying to take control of ports while their noblemen squabble. All of these attacks are like … warning shots." Tomaso's eyes moved back to the mirror. His pale, scared reflection stared back at him.

Gilulia leant forward, her long, thin fingers plucking at a sliver of fish. She popped it into her mouth and shook her head. "Too much salt. You should have said something, Tomaso."

"I only just found out!"

"No, about the salt," Gilulia said, slipping deeper into her chair. It looked as if she might disappear completely into the depths of the ageing armchair. "I had my suspicions about the government's deceit. The Reflections told me as much. Still, it's nice to receive confirmation that one isn't suffering from late-set paranoia. I just wish I could say I was surprised. But honestly, if you give a man a fish a day, he's quickly thinking of how to drain the entire ocean."

"But you're still going to help, right? You can't just leave us defenceless; you wouldn't let us all burn, would you?" The words flew out of Tomaso at such speed he was amazed they were even in the right order. His insides clenched, waiting for an answer. The weight of thousands of lives pressed down on him. If Gilulia wouldn't help because he told her, if people died because of him…

Gilulia rubbed the bridge of her nose. Tomaso counted the seconds of silence in his head, the number growing higher, the weight on his shoulder growing heavier. When she finally moved her hand away, her emerald green eyes meeting his, he felt his chest tighten. All the stress of the last several months unfurled and threatened to barrel him down.

"Oh, don't be dramatic. Of course, I'll help. Someone has to stop this madness before those idiots wipe out a plank of our city. I just won't be killing any more Turks either. Foolish of me, to lash out before doing my own investigations. That's old age for you, I suppose. So set in my ways that I didn't bother to think." Gilulia reached for another slice of fish. Somehow, she seemed older than ever, a dozen new lines creasing her already riddled forehead. "You'll be sent to the front lines, will you?"

"I guess so."

"I best give you a few things in case my spells go awry. I've grown quite fond of you, Private da Guda," Gilulia said and Tomaso looked at his feet, feeling a warmth fill his cheeks. "Go on, eat up. I'll be back in a moment."

Alone in the attic, Tomaso stared at the meal in front of him. He didn't see the fish or the plate it sat on. All he could see, the image wrestling its way to the front of his mind, was the sight of a battlefield. So concerned with Gilulia and her betrayal, he hadn't stopped to think what the encroaching army meant for him. He was a soldier. Soldiers fought other men who came to burn their city. The Venetian Army was for decoration, though. The Glassblower's Peace saw to that. Now Tomaso had a chance to fight, a chance of glory. He felt his stomach churn. He had watched those ships burn that night in the glass gondola. Even without fighting, he knew there was no such thing as a glorious death. Still, the idea of desertion never crossed his mind. Gilulia would do something. He knew it with the same conviction he had when they confronted the Ottoman flotilla several months ago.

Gilulia reappeared in the attic, a laden tray in her hands. The objects glinted in the light. As she walked closer, Tomaso could make out the shapes of the glass in front of him: a long sword and a small pendant on a silver chain. They were beautiful. The blade of the sword curved, the glass as blue as the sea. In the pendant, buried in the crystal-clear glass, was a tiny black cat. Frozen in time, the cat looked as if it was poised to jump at some unseen bird.

"The sword isn't much better than steel, I'm afraid. A little sharper, a little stronger, a little deadlier. Might be good at cutting through any carpets," Gilulia said as Tomaso grabbed the sword by its handle. It pulsed against his palm. "Keep the pendant safe, though. Make sure it's touching your skin. Under the shirt, not over it. Remember that."

* * *

An army encampment had a constant hum, audible even over the roaring of a storm. Thousands of men, all of them terrified of not seeing next week, drank and drank until sobriety seemed like a distant memory. Laughter and vulgar songs filled the air. The relentless noise began to crawl beneath Tomaso's skin. He was completely sober, too afraid to drink in case the pendant somehow slipped from his neck. The sword had disappeared as soon as General di Barso saw it at his hip, commandeering it to someone who deserved it more: namely, the General. Picking up his pack, Tomaso decided to strike out for the hill overlooking the encampment. At least there, he might have a moment of peace.

Instead, the wind whistled louder. He hid beneath the branches of a great oak. It offered him a little comfort from the rain. There was an odd contradiction that something capable of so much death like an army could look so beautiful, but looking down at the encampment, the golden yellow hues of lanterns swaying across the countryside, Tomaso found the scene breathtaking. If he was Gilulia, perhaps he could have found a way to freeze the entire moment and then do the same to the Ottoman army, ensuring peace. He wasn't Gilulia though. All he could do was try not to cry as the rain fell around him, nearly failing to notice that the raindrops dripping from the leaves of the oak were not raindrops at all. They were tiny crystal shards. Landing on the soft, wet grass, the glass pooled into a puddle and Tomaso stumbled to his feet, his chest tightening. Each individual shard melted together, a perfect mirror forming in front of him. A figure eased his way out of the glass.

A dark-skinned man was standing in front of him, a neatly tied beard reaching down to his chest. "Ah, I was expecting Madame Seguso. Are you an apprentice of hers?"

"Not exactly…" Tomaso said, letting the answer drift off, unsure what title to give to the Arab.

"Emir Mehmed at your service," the man said, dipping his head just an inch. "I assume you are to explain the exact nature of the Ottoman army's current predicament?"

Tomaso froze, even his shivering from the cold going deathly still. Gilulia had told him about the Vizier of Sorcery. He wasn't sure if he should try and stab him or answer his question, and Tomaso found himself unable to do either. Fortunately, another figure was pulling themselves free from the glass puddle. His uniform was grand and there was a glass sword at his hip. Tomaso swallowed thickly, General di Barso standing in front of him.

"Private da Guda, what is the meaning of this?" Every possible horrible conclusion flickered across the General's eyes. Tomaso didn't care anymore. Blood still boiling at Gilulia's treatment, he opened his mouth, ready to unload upon his ranking officer.

"The private is just as clueless as yourself, General," a voice echoed from the puddle.

A curious ripple of reaction travelled through the three men standing on the rain-sodden hill above the Venetian army. Tomaso felt his spirits soared at Gilulia's voice; she was about to reveal some glorious plan that was going to save the day. General di Barso meanwhile cringed and took a step away from the puddle as if some hand might emerge from it and slap him hard across the cheek. His hand dropped to the glass sword, trying to hide it from view. Emir Mehmed merely snorted.

"Will you not be joining us, Madame Seguso?" Mehmed bowed deeply to the puddle.

"Not today, Emir," it spoke in Gilulia's unmistakable voice. "I don't travel through such small quantities of glass. It gives me indigestion."

The General stiffened, the crease in his brow becoming more permanent with every passing second. "Seguso, what are you doing talking so … so civilly to such a man? First, you refuse to aid our army and now you consult with our enemy. I'll have you brought before the Doge."

"Unlike soldiers and politicians, the magicians of the world do not remain so solidly in their little bubbles so as to not engage in correspondence with their equals. Regardless, it was necessary to bring two emissaries together for me to explain my spell. There'll be no misunderstandings. I trust the Emir's judgement to explain Venice's new position to the Grand Vizier and the Sultan. I trust you to shut up or that sword on your belt will shred your manhood with a thousand shards," the puddle said.

The Emir lowered his head in respect and Tomaso took a step

back into the embrace of the oak, hiding as the General's face grew splotchier. "What spell?" he said, trying to slide the sword off his belt. It didn't budge.

"There will be no battle," the puddle declared. "If you both agree to my terms, there will even be no war. Emir, in case you hadn't worked it out, your forces are currently lost somewhere in northern Russia. I advise marching home as quickly as possible; it's awfully cold there, I hear. If you continue insisting on attacking Venice, you'll find yourself deposited in various places across the globe. I can't promise all of them will be as near to Constantinople as Russia."

"These are not so much terms as threats, Madame."

"Let me finish, Emir. The spell holding you back from Venice will only continue to exist if its government ceases to attack the outlying Ottoman ports. If these attacks continue, I will pull down the enchantments and Venice will be left defenceless. I do hope you'll behave yourself, General, or things will get awfully messy."

The General bristled at the puddle. "You're overstepping your bounds, Seguso. You're a servant of the Venetian government; you're not its Queen."

"I tender my resignation, you old fool," Giulia's voice echoed. Tomaso gasped, but the two other men ignored him. "You used my magic for greed. You don't deserve my protection anymore, and I don't deserve my position. I'm getting old and too set in my ways. I'll be gone before you're back in the city. Live in peace or gamble that this inexperienced rabble you call an army can withhold the Turks and young Emir here. I don't fancy your chances."

"I won't," the General said, taking a step forward as if he

could somehow intimidate the puddle. An invisible line wrapped around his body and flung him toward the opening, the glass swallowing him whole.

"Well, Madame Seguso," Mehmed said, also stepping toward the puddle. "I'll return to my army, if you please. And I will lead them home. I hope Venice obeys by your terms; we have no desire to burn such a beautiful city." He nodded at Tomaso and then dived into the puddle.

Tomaso stood alone on the hill. The wind whipped at his exposed skin, the rain mingling with the tears running down his face. Relief and despair coursed through his veins in equal measure, a sickening mixture as he sagged back against the embrace of the oak tree. The war was over, he knew it. Venice could never truly risk an actual war with the Ottomans. They would have to cower behind the Glassblower's final protection, a true peace. Yet Gilulia would be gone from the city and again with that deep, well-earthed conviction, Tomaso knew he would never see her again.

"Are you still there, Tomaso?" Gilulia's voice sounded further away now, leaving the puddle far quieter.

"Yes," Tomaso said, pushing the word through the wall in his throat. He stumbled closer to the glass still pooled on the ground. A goodbye was coming and he didn't want to hear it. Somehow the pain throbbing larger in his chest hurt more than anything he had felt for his parents' death. "How did you send them to Russia?"

"Glass, Tomaso. Always just glass. A lot of it, though. It'll take me a long time to restock my supplies. Maybe I won't bother."

"I could help."

The puddle laughed. "Glassblowing is an art, boy. And magic

is a science. You can't pick up either without years, maybe decades of practice. No, you can't help, Tomaso. It's the way of life, and you've got another life to live. Enjoy it this time. Embrace it. Don't dwell on old things like me."

"They took your sword." Tomaso didn't know what else to say. The longer the conversation continued, the longer Gilulia would be there to talk to.

"As I expected. You still have the pendant, though, don't you, Tomaso? You'd never give that away, promise me," Gilulia said through the puddle. Tomaso pressed his fingers to his chest, feeling the lump beneath his shirt. "You keep hold of that and everything will work out. I'll see to that. Goodbye, Tomaso da Guda."

"Goodbye, Gilulia."

* * *

As soon as he arrived back in the city, Tomaso headed to the Ghetto. Gilulia's house was gone, replaced with a large glass tower. It was no artistic masterpiece. An opaque, harsh block reached up to the sky, dominating the courtyard. There had been a small band of soldiers stood in front of the glass structure, General di Barso red-faced, yelling behind them. The men struck out at the tower with their blades, steel hammering against glass. They left no marks; the tower untouched. Tomaso slipped away, back toward San Croce. He hoped Gilulia was out of the glass tower, perhaps on some French holiday instead of slaving over a kiln. He suppressed a snort as he imagined the old woman lying on some sandy beach.

Turning a corner into his street, Tomaso spied a man sitting on his doorstep at the other end of the street. The pendant against his skin seemed to grow warmer. His muscles tensed, ready to run. Then the man shifted, a leathery, tanned face looking back at him and he offered Tomaso a wave. Someone who wanted to do him harm probably wouldn't hail him, and the gentle pulsing of the pendant suddenly seemed more like a cat's purring.

"Tomaso?" The man said. Tomaso nodded and the man offered him his hand. His green eyes seemed to fight to meet Tomaso's. "I'm Marco." Tomaso remembered meeting the man in a tavern on one occasion, an orphan who turned to the sea for a family. "I … I was a crew mate of your brother."

A year ago, the past tense would have bowled him over, knocking the air right out of his lungs. Since he had walked into Gilulia's house for the first time, though, and heard the wind chimes' melodies, Tomaso knew his brother was dead. He nodded at Marco and relieved him of his obligation of speaking the words aloud. "Thank you for coming. I appreciate the visit."

"You're one of the few," Marco said, standing a little taller as if a weight had been lifted from his body. "Everyone else wishes that I had taken the place of their loved one." The words unspoken: who would miss some orphan boy?

"Why don't you come in?" Tomaso barrelled through any objections, opening the door. He saw the same darkness hidden behind Marco's eyes as he felt behind his own. A crushing loneliness that had to be pushed back if someone was to truly embrace life. "You can tell me some stories about my brother and I can offer you a meal. It's the least I can do."

The pendant around Tomaso's neck purred in approval.

MIRROR MIRROR
MARK ENGLISH

I pretend an interest in the dusky view through the train window, but I am focussed utterly on my reflection. I wonder if my vitreous shade can still hear Martin's screams echoing in her head, feel the weight of his limbs in her hands, and bear the guilt as do I.

I stare at my mirror-self, which in turn critically appraises me. I wait to see if she twitches in the window, but instead she matches my non-blinking stare, her face a closed door to the secrets we must not divulge.

In the seat across from me, my guard looks up from his newspaper as the sliding grind of the first-class carriage door, accompanied by the rush of track and corridor noises, heralds the return of his colleague.

I observe their reflections as I stare at the train window. They exchange glances: a raised brow, a head shake. A line wrinkles in the corner of my eye as I focus on imagining they are not really with me, but exist only in the reflection: with *her*. My ears hear them, reporting the lie; the illusion breaks.

The guards change positions and the new arrival takes on the stewardship of the newspaper. He shakes it out as the first guard leaves the carriage. I see the headline. News of my husband's 'defection' is still being reported despite a security clampdown. I should be thankful – if not for the leak I would have been disappeared in the same 'accident' and fire that destroyed my lab. As a news item I am more titillating than the Cold War. From what I have read, I can see that there is one truth for the people and another for the military.

The real truth comes back to me in shards and slivers – this I keep for myself.

* * *

Years of research, applications for grants and sheer elbow grease stood assembled before us. In many ways a structure of great beauty – winding copper coils, coolant valves, power cabling, and a full-height silvered mirror as the centre piece. I fancied it as the fairytale mirror from Snow White captured by science into an iron frame. The summer sun through the hangar windows sparkled on the machine; a cold, glittering readiness.

The deepening frost in the Cold War had compressed our schedule. The weekly reviews became daily reviews, and very firm. The increased military presence on each review board brought a gritty reality to the pure research dream. We wanted to demonstrate the use of parallel universes as a method of transport. The demand to show results pushed us to deliver early.

I wound my arms around Martin's waist, poked my head over his shoulder and gazed at the sum of our efforts.

"Pity it doesn't work." I bobbed my chin against his bony shoulder and squinted at his profile. A stray hair escaped my headscarf, tickling my cheek; I puffed it away.

"Yup. Perhaps it needs more power, Jean." He attempted to

move towards the distribution box.

"No. We are looking at a weak effect – the evanescent wave on the mirror is already in place, showing light from the mirror dimension." I tightened my grip, squeezing a cough from him. "This is Everett's many worlds hypothesis made real – exactly as per my theories!"

The view in the mirror was not a reflection; a reciprocal world shone into ours. The pitch to the research board seemed so long ago – the proposal to move matter across the interface and bring it back through a different mirror.

The military heard about it – only they had seen more and further. They grasped the potential to bring another army over from the mirror dimension, to borrow and reinforce from that universe, or materialise an atomic bomb anywhere. Deep in the science as we were, we had greeted news of the military funding with a mix of horrified disquiet and blinkered excitement.

"Perhaps the mirror isn't smooth enough?" he queried, twisting his neck to face me. He puffed at the stray hair also, his efforts making me blink.

"No." I smiled at him. "I think it doesn't work because we don't want it to." He knew what I meant.

"Well, I want it to work just so we know you were right." A smile wrinkled his cheek.

I moved my mouth close to his ear, to breathe my response. "You know very well we haven't applied the Everett field pattern to the mirror yet. However, I took the precaution of blacking out the security cameras. What say we get this baby rocking? Then we could take it to pieces and burn all the notes. Though we'd probably live out our lives in prison, at least we'd be together."

He wriggled in my locked arms, turned and hugged me back.

He leaned in to me, his breath tickling my ear, "Okay, you minx, let's pull Frankenstein's lever."

I pushed myself from his arms and semi-danced across the concrete floor to the bulb-ridden control panel. I pulled a fuse from my trouser pocket, waggled it at him playfully, lifted a hatch on the panel and slipped the fuse in place. I dithered my hand over the switch.

If this worked, we would have to destroy our notes; this machine would be horrendous as a weapon. If it did not work, it would be a relief on the one hand, but I knew my failure would shake me – deeply.

My face started tingling as the doubts mounted, I could see a shake in my hand. I glanced at Martin, imploring him for reassurance, but he held back knowing this moment was mine.

A smile cracked his rigid expression, "Breathe, Jean, breathe."

I inhaled deeply, blinking away the dots that began dancing before my eyes. With a loud yell I gulped air, and slammed the switch home.

A high pitched whine dashed around the vaulting of the hangar, fading to a sibilant hiss as the coils started building to their peak. A few minutes and I would know the truth.

* * *

I woke to a sharp stinging pain in my cheek, the odour of burnt hair, and the abrasive calls of approaching sirens. A blurred face loomed over me, yelling. Strong hands shook me.

"Where is your husband? How did the fire start? Where are your notes?"

The words washed through me as the face snapped into focus,

security-standard mirrored sunglasses reflecting back an image of the woman, unharmed. Me. I sobbed at the evidence of a loose end.

"He's gone. Forever. All gone, all burned."

The sirens stopped. Running feet approached. Medics pushed my interrogator roughly aside and lifted me onto a stretcher. I lapsed back into a blurry unconsciousness.

* * *

The coils took a few minutes to fill with the terrible charge required to trick the universe. It would take same time for the Everett field to collapse once the power was turned off.

Martin and I scarcely breathed, the seconds interminable until the circuits clicked over and the full charge was applied to the mirror.

Air moved past me chilling my skin like a fresh breeze, I checked over my shoulder to see if a window were open. The mirrored surface roiled like hot oil in a frying-pan, cells of silver expanding out, clashing with each other then shrinking back down again. We stepped towards the surface, entranced by the eldritch sheen, trying to observe any differences between worlds; anything that would tell us we could slide matter into their world without a change in ours.

Our reflections gaped back at us, identical. The math must be correct; with the uncertainty applied to the evanescent wave there should be minute, visible differences.

The reflections ducked and weaved, matching our own jerky motions as we tried to catch sight of any delay in movement. There was nothing visible.

We both stepped forward cautiously. Martin reached out, tentatively poised to touch his image.

"Look at it Jean – just as you predicted," his hand wavered in front of the mercurial sheen, "but why is the Everett shift not visible to us?"

"Back away Martin, I may have got the order of magnitude wrong." Even as the last word left my lips and faded into a hush, his fingertip came to rest on the phantom surface. It was a gentle motion, tender as a touch on a lover's neck.

That fragment of time locked itself in my memory. Within one breath my intellectual conquest would be realised. Without trying, I can take my mind back to that moment: dust motes speared by light in the air between Martin and his shifting re-flection, his chin and neck stubble, the skin under his eyes dark from the long days building to my designs.

That quantum of time I now see as a meniscus between our life together and the ensuing madness of absolute loss. My chest thudded once, hard, my heart kicking off with the dump of adrenaline, and time rolled onward.

* * *

The nurse sat on the foot of my bed, clean, precise, smiling. "How are we doing?"

I pointed to the television that burbled to itself on a trolley in the corner. "Could you turn that off, please, and bring it here next to my bed?"

The nurse frowned as though being helpful were an affront, but did so, wheeling the now reflective screen closer. I turned away from her and gazed at my new bedside companion.

"How're we doing?" I repeated. "We've been abandoned and burned." I lifted a hand, moved it back and forth rapidly, staring into the screen. "What a dumb question."

The nurse stood and left, her figure retreating deeper into the screen's dark interior.

* * *

Martin pressed his finger firmly into the mirror. "My reflection is tracking me, Jean, so looks like we'll get crossover."

I expected Martin to pass through the surface and join his reflection. It appeared we were getting the second predicted result – Martin and his reverse twin exchanging through the interface. Neither of us foresaw a third possible solution to the field equations.

Martin's finger progressed inwards, but did not appear in the reciprocal view of the mirror. The surface swallowed his fingertip like liquid mercury, disappearing under the surface. He did not appear in the reflection, and nothing came out into our world.

Martin wrenched his arm, trying to pull back, rocking the iron-framed mirror. "Jean! My finger is stuck, like concrete. I can't feel anything from it."

I leaped forward and grasped his elbow as the roiling silver swallowed his hand. I pulled back with all my weight – to no avail. He was locked in place. I dashed to the control panel and opened the switch. The coils emitted a contented, languorous, malevolent sigh.

Nearly tripping in heart-thudding haste, I grabbed back at Martin's arm. In the seconds I stood at the control panel he had sunken to the elbow on his right arm. His left, braced bloodless and straining against the frame, must have touched the flowing metal; the silver drew it in. I grabbed his shoulders, jammed my foot against the frame and pulled back, hard.

My legs and arms shook. Martin shrieked, eyes wide, face paling as his reflection sucked him into a terminal embrace. In the oil-on-water calm of the mirror, our counterparts writhed and screamed with us, every movement and scuffle matched in synchronicity.

Martin sobbed as his fringe touched the metal. He ripped his head back, leaving hairs standing proud of the mirror. He stared as they wriggled, turning and shortening as though drilling their way into the silver. "Jean, stop pulling me – it's no good. By the time the coils dissipate, I, I … it will be too late for me."

I hugged him around the waist and kissed his cheek, a dark parody of earlier. "Minutes, that's all we need, just minutes. It could stop at any time now." My tears rose up, choking my throat as the adrenaline ebbed.

He turned his head to kiss me back. "I know … I know how much this work means to you, but this device is not what you described. Now let me go, before you get sucked in too."

I released him. The cooling breeze from the mirror sucking in the atmosphere left a chill on my arms. A breathy warning from the deadly surface.

Martin arched his back, his arms sunk to the shoulders, holding himself away as long as possible. "Jean, destroy this! Destroy it before it gets abused. Destroy our notes, everything."

My mind washed over with white, then burned red as my breathing sped up; Martin was disappearing, my husband, my partner, my balance in the world.

"No!" I jumped forward, grabbing at the clothes on his back, pulling uselessly as he pitched forward, his face touching the metal. The machine drew him in as though desperate to finish him with the last ebbing charge. I grasped his ankles, felt his legs spasm then fall still as his head passed across the shining veil. I could see my counter self, hands grasping ankles that led to limbs that led to me. Tears tracked from unblinking eyes, crossing her bloodless cheeks.

The coils ceased their whining as Martin's knees passed through the surface. I stared at the other woman, at the other end of the other legs. I knew the mirror dimension existed, and that she looked at me with the same shaking lips and dazed expression as I displayed to her.

Without the support of the negating mirror, Martin's limbs gathered weight. The truncated remains slid down the shining stilled surface, trailing blood.

The feel of the heavy dead flesh of my lover in my hands, the bloody tracks before me, whirled my vision. A dark wave rushed through my mind like a blow to the head, not hard not violent, but muted and muting. It took me like a rip-tide, whirled me around, swept me out of sight, out of mind.

Moments may have passed, or hours. I struggled up from the floor to stand and look at the gruesome evidence. The blood-streaked mirror, the remains of my Martin. I stepped up to my reflection, placed my hand on the cold, quiescent surface, touching glacial palms with my new heart-bound partner.

"I'm sorry for your loss. He was a good man." I saw her lips move, but heard my voice.

Martin was no longer in either universe. Could you go to heaven if your soul was erased? I shuddered. Everything must be destroyed. I looked back to my collaborator. We both accepted the task before us. Martin was dead; it all had to go. It would all burn, but there must be no evidence of neatly excised bones or any notion that the machine had been run. The woman in the mirror straightened her shoulders and nodded encouragingly at me.

I crossed to the machine and started it up; the coils sighed back into life. While they charged I gathered my notebooks and all the designs, then sat waiting for the surface to boil into life.

The charge swept across the surface with a sharp click – my cue to feed the documents into the shining void. Once the paper was consumed, I gently lifted Martin's legs, their cold weight impressing into my memory.

I flicked my gaze to my reflection, then we sent our lover's remains on their final voyage.

"See you soon, Martin," we chanted in unison, grief-matched faces across the metal haze. We felt the draw to launch into oblivion, be removed from this loss; but the machine had to be destroyed. This would not be our way out. We turned our machines off, waved au revoir.

Together we took fire-axes to all electronics and cabling, then swept the remains into a pile at the base of the mirror. Stepping onto the wreckage, I watched the figure in the glass douse herself in ethanol from a flagon, shaking it liberally above her head and over the stacked remnants of her experiment. The scene leapt brightly as I saw her flick a cigarette lighter to yellow life. A second later, the room lit with the blue ghosts of ethanol flame that danced over her body and the heaped machinery. I saw her gasp, drawing blue flame into her mouth. I screamed, and crumpled in pain as I saw her sag into unconscious bliss.

* * *

The huddle of doctors outside my door clearly did not care what I heard. Their conversation wafted quietly into my room.

"All she does is stare at that blank screen, and now and again she will move a hand or foot. The defection, and brutal attempted murder, has scrambled her. In my opinion she is no longer any use to the programme."

They questioned me many times. Could I tell them what had gone on? I could not explain to them without revealing the results of the experiment, or Martin's fate. I kept my own counsel. My eyes sought out the dead television to draw solidarity from the friendly gaze of my sister in silence.

They asked if Martin had defected, gone over to the other side? They meant the Russians, but this question threw me into a violent hysterical fit. The ensuing struggling spasms always resulted in sedation. I grew to welcome the needle-sharp announcement of the stupefiers.

From the questions they asked, I gleaned that they had recovered nothing. They had no idea the machine worked, and there were no records of my theories.

My survival from the fire became a closely guarded secret. If not for the leak to the press about the 'scientist defection', I am sure I would have been taken somewhere discreet, and both Martin and I accounted for in the inferno that destroyed the lab.

It was decided that I was to spend time out of contact, somewhere I could be guarded and coaxed back to sanity.

Sanity.

My silence on all fronts left me open to many interpretations, none of which bothered me. I turned to check my dark reflection – she smiled at me knowingly and winked. Neither of us were bothered.

* * *

The woman in the train window smiled grimly at me as the pastoral scenes slid past under a glowering sky. We would be having time in the country. In the words of our psychologist – time to reflect.

COMMON DENOMINATOR
MELANIE HARDING-SHAW

When I first met my latest ex, 'Sultans of Swing' by Dire Straits was belting out of the speakers and I had to wipe my hands before I danced with him because the bar was so sticky from spilled beer. That dance set up a false expectation for our relationship, although the bar itself should have tipped me off. I wonder what my chip would have played that night if I'd had it back then. Maybe 'Luka' by Suzanne Vega.

He was just the latest in a series of poor choices on my part. Each time, I swear that the next time will be different. But it never is – I don't know how to be different. I am the common denominator in my relationships. Maybe they're my own fault.

When they asked for volunteers to beta test a media chip implanted in your brain I was first in line, although the queue wasn't exactly stretching around the block. The promise of music played directly to my auditory cortex in response to my emotions was too tempting to refuse. I don't deserve much but I had always known my messed-up life deserved its own soundtrack.

The chip didn't disappoint. When I was depressed, it played something I couldn't help but dance to. When I was angry, it mellowed me out. Soon everybody with money had one. I would never have been able to afford one myself.

I was sitting at a bar the first time it happened. A guy came and leaned beside me. He was wearing a white-collared shirt with the top two buttons undone so I had to keep pulling my eyes back up to his face, and he smelled like clean clothes and money. He was looking at the chip controller on my wrist.

"You don't see many of those around here," he said with a smooth smile. He pulled his sleeve up a little and put his wrist next to mine to compare. "Yours looks like a newer model." His fingers brushed mine as he pulled his sleeve back down.

I smiled into his blue eyes, "Yeah, I'm a tester. This upgrade hasn't been released yet." I would have carried on, maybe asked him to dance, but 'Smooth Criminal' by Michael Jackson started playing in my mind so loud that it drowned out every other sound in the bar. I winced and rubbed my temples and the volume went down a little.

"Are you OK? Can I buy you a drink?" the guy asked.

Was I OK? I wasn't sure. The chip was not supposed to do that. "No thanks, I need to go sorry." I grabbed my coat from the stool next to me.

"Here's my card. Give me a call when you're feeling better," he said. As he helped me put my coat on, his hands ran down my arms and I trembled a little. Was I being silly? The chip was designed to respond to my emotions and the only thing I was feeling was horny, it must be defective. He was beautiful and clearly successful. He was nothing like my ex-boyfriends. The volume of 'Smooth Criminal' went back up. The common denominator in my relationships is me. I left without him.

I had to report the incident to the developers of course.

Playing loud music while you're at a bar listening to loud music is not what the chips are supposed to do. I knew something was wrong when they didn't let me leave. Instead I was interviewed by progressively more and more senior people at the company. No-one was telling me what was going on, but I could kind of tell what the problem was. "Were your controllers still touching when the music started? Did they try and sync with each other?"

No, they didn't, not that I noticed anyway. But I guess my chip was reading something from his chip or they wouldn't be asking. When I finally got home I trawled the internet for anything about the guy. He was a high-flying investment banker. I used the email address on his card to find his Facebook page, wondering if I should send him a friend request just to get access. His privacy settings were locked right down and everything else was corporate vanilla.

A folk guitar intro started playing in my mind and I looked down at my controller in surprise – 'Whisper Your Mother's Name' by Jimmie Rodgers. I hit the stop button, it really wasn't my thing. The chip was definitely defective. As soon as I took my hand away it started playing again. My finger hovered over the stop button. Would the developers have been so worried if it was just a defect though?

I looked again at the Facebook login screen in front of me and then touched the back of my neck, where the chip had been implanted, with shaking hands. It only took a moment of searching his friends list to figure out who his mother was. I typed her name into the password field and was rewarded with full access to his page and messages.

He was too clever to put anything incriminating on Facebook messenger but the signs were clear for someone with my history.

He looked different to my exes on the outside, but inside he was just the same. He was an abusive predator and he had at least three women on the hook.

The developers left me five messages the next day asking me to come in and have the chip removed. I looked around my dirty apartment, breathed in the smog from the diesel trains that ran below my window, and I packed a bag and left. 'Cold War' by Janelle Monae was the soundtrack of my escape. Was I alone?

I am the common denominator in my relationships. That is my super power. I'm not a victim any more. The chip and I can tell if you're going to beat me, or worse. Together, we can do something about it.

THE PEOPLE BETWEEN THE SILENCES
DAVE MOORE

If I tell her this one last thing about me, I'll probably lose her. But I probably will anyway if I say nothing, so I can't keep quiet anymore.

I know Min is it, because I've been around long enough to recognise when people are good for each other. And she has too. We don't say it out loud, but we both know that this is the one we don't mess up. She mustn't see me as too damaged or weird for her because she doesn't need any more of that. When she sees that she walks.

It's been good. Almost three years and we are steady, practical people now. There's the business. We get up in the morning when we know we should, and we get on and do the things we need to do until they are done. We do life properly – for ourselves, and even more for each other. Because we've tried the other way and it didn't work.

I've been famous most of my life for fucking up perfectly good things that looked impossible to derail. And she's been far too good at putting up with men like me who all did that. But we met clean, Min and I, stepping out of our own trails of wreckage. We found each other that day, and told the truth. We made a little window of light.

"Honesty – it's at the heart of you and I," she always says, and she's right. But I hug her quickly at that moment so she can't see my eyes.

I haven't killed anyone. I've done nothing dramatic or illegal. I just see things; I see people. People who shouldn't be there. Not all the time, or every day. I can't explain because I don't understand it myself. But she would assume it was a hangover from the drugs and booze. She grew up with that shit all around and she's had enough for one lifetime, and fair enough.

So if I told her I saw things sometimes that other people didn't, she wouldn't attack me or anything, or invite the drug squad in to turn the place over. But she would walk away. Because she's learned to do that, and look at her now – you can see she's right. She's strong and doing it right. Because she's learned to leave instead of maiming herself trying to save all the broken people around her.

So anyway, what happens is that I will see someone, just out, like anyone else. But there will be something about them that doesn't look right. Often it's their clothes I notice first. On a day warm enough for just a t-shirt, they might have on a jumper and jacket too – but not look bothered by being so overdressed. Or I might pass them out walking on a muddy track, but in clean shoes. Then they disappear.

When I got to 19 or 20 and finally accepted what was going on, I got brave and started speaking to them. Mostly about the place, about the day, the weather. They can't generally talk about anything else, and it bothers them if I ask. They turn away. It's called audiovoyance or something when you can hear and speak to them as well as see them. I think that's it, but I don't look into it or ask around.

I don't think it's from a smack on the head – falling over pub steps or coming off the bike or getting coat-hangered. Because I saw these people before that, when I was a kid. I just didn't admit it back then.

I've told a couple of mates but only when I knew they were pissed enough not to remember in the morning. Because it's not the sort of thing I wanted people talking about, about me. Especially not to Min.

When she was about 14 or 15, maybe even younger, she had this boy she really liked. He was pretty sensible I think, doing better than most at school – like her, and I can imagine the two of them planning how they would get out and do everything differently. He had an elder brother who always had drugs, but this lad, the one she was with, he kept away.

One night though, when he was watching the footy upstairs with his brother and a few older mates, just for a laugh they stuck a tab of acid in his drink when he was fetching more chips.

Their mother came home later and looked up and saw him stood there balancing on the balustrading over the stairwell talking to himself. She couldn't get there in time to stop him diving like he was bungy jumping or hang gliding or something. He only fell one floor but there was lots to hit on the way down.

They cleared him from hospital after a few weeks, saying there was nothing wrong now – he was all fixed. But he wasn't. Apparently he wasn't the same bloke anymore. Either the head injury or the LSD had changed some wiring. And Min didn't like the new one, the lying bastard they sent home. Few people did.

She had too many around her like that, over the years. Different drugs, but similar stories and the same endings. And then there were the usual social drinkers with too many friends. Like I used to be. Bright enough to find reasons to do the wrong things day after day, until all the good things have gone, including the memory.

Min was like her mother – a carer. She cared for everybody, but there were too many of them. Finally, the twat from Geelong did a runner with just about everything she had. That Christmas she went for a lie-down at her mum's after lunch and didn't get up again properly until they were writing the cards for the next one. The doctors called it various things, but Abby never saw it as medical. She just put her daughter on a "love drip", as she called it. Kept away the damaged and needy who drained her, and let the girl slowly put enough back in the tank to stand again. When she re-joined the world it was on different terms. It had to be.

* * *

I would talk to our doc if I could guarantee she'd say I was solid. But I don't want to risk the visit leading to bad stuff. Because it's never felt like it's something wrong with me. When I look at google it says hallucinations can happen when the body is highly stressed, like mountaineers or people running races across the desert. But it doesn't feel like that. When the army and I were still an item, I got so shattered alone on one night exercise that by the early morning I couldn't read the map or see the track to take – even though it was right in front of me. I sat myself down for a few minutes by a lake and drank and ate what I had left. Within minutes everything became obvious and normal again.

But I didn't see anyone who shouldn't have been there, and

that deprivation felt completely different. Being tired beyond words shut things down in me, whereas when I see these people I feel like it's because how I see the world has opened further up. That's all I can say really, because like I said I don't understand it. There is a silence around them, but otherwise I am more aware, not less. And I've got used to it.

Mostly it's when I'm on foot, but once I saw someone in a car on the motorway. He appeared alongside me driving a 1990s faded blue Toyota or Nissan, and stayed there for a few minutes. A young guy, worried about something, looking straight ahead with dark, scared eyes. After a while he eased back behind me and I watched him in the mirrors. Then as he went through my blind spot he disappeared. There was no exit nearby and the road was clear behind me for a kilometre or two.

I've seen Min do it – shut off and cut people out when she feels she must. The daughter of an old friend of hers asked to crash on the sofa bed last summer. Just for a couple of nights. When she arrived I went and got a takeaway and this girl – Bel – produced a load of wine, drank most of it, and as the evening went on she started talking about her mate who could tell you your past lives, and how she'd been sceptical but now believed it. She'd been told she could do it too, she had the gift, and said she had already picked things up about us. So she just started coming out with stuff about me and about Min.

I knew Bel's mum had lost a few years to drugs at that age and as we listened to this weird shit getting weirder, both of us wondered about her girl. Her eyes weren't right. And she said things you don't say to people you barely know. I didn't argue or anything, I mean, who am I to say what's real and what isn't? But when Bel got onto how miscarriages – we've had two – were often punishments carried over from previous lives, but that she could take us to meet their souls, Min just got up, went out the back and rang Bel's mum. When she came back in Min just told her to pack and go, and stood watching until she did. It was dark and getting late and I gave her taxi money and a bit extra because I felt bad.

So I know how definite she is now, Min.

* * *

Today was different for me. In all the years I've seen these people they have always been strangers. Never someone I knew. But this morning Min's mum died.

At about ten or a bit after, but I didn't know that. Nor did Min straightaway, because she was at ours still doing the GST before going up to the Home to see her. And at about that time I was stopped at the lights, looked across and saw Abby, Min's mum, in her favourite coat and hat at her old bus stop in Hataitai waiting to go through the tunnel into town. She had her work-bag and was stood enjoying the sun, looking like she did before the fall. I watched her for a few seconds but she didn't look my way, and then the lights changed and by the time I could pull out of the traffic and go back she wasn't there anymore.

Instead of going back to the job in Newtown I just headed round, got on the motorway at The Terrace and went slowly towards the Home where she'd been since the op. I didn't know what to do but this felt right. I didn't call Min because there was nothing I could say. I was just waiting and hoping.

I was just before Petone when the phone rang in my jacket in the back of the cab. I let it go to message, because it would have been unusual if I didn't when I was supposed to be working. Min just said the Home had called and could I come straightaway and meet her there. I pulled into Petone and drove down the waterfront to kill time. I sat and watched the ferry heading out and thought about Abby. We'd got on well, me and her mum. And I was proud of that, because it was a first for me – having a mother see me as someone who could care for her girl.

As I sat there a friend of hers came slowly past with her dog. There was nowhere to hide and she'd have known the truck anyway. We spoke for a minute and then I drove off to the Home.

Min saw me arrive just as she was walking in. I had got there too fast from the job at that time of day. She asked why but I offered no excuse because I'm a crap liar. And then I just couldn't look surprised and empty enough when she told me what the nurses had said.

When she and I sat with the body I could tell my reaction was all wrong. I was just too prepared, one or two steps on, but how could she know that? Min just looked at me, confused for a while and then suspicious and then deeply hurt, and I saw something start to switch off behind her eyes. This woman I need utterly was looking at yet another man who had either been pretending to be honest with her all along – or was pretending now. It amounted to the same.

And so right here I need to explain about this last part of me. Because she's going to walk.

TE IKA

J.C. HART

IZZY

I did not want to go.

The black maw of the hole did not beckon to me. If anything, it urged me to run, to throw down my caving gear and get back in the car, to speed towards town and the safety of buildings and streets and lights and noise. It was too quiet here, too still, even with the occasional bird lifting its voice in song.

"Izzy," Grace urged. "Come on. We don't want to leave it too long. We've got to be home in time for the family dinner." She hovered at the edge of the cave, helmet on and her harness in place. She looked better in the rig than I ever would, but then, she was the pro and I was just the tag-along. That summed up our whole life.

"Whose idea was this anyway?" I asked, rolling my eyes.

"Mum wanted you to get out more. You said you'd give it a go." Grace put her hands on her hips and gave me the same glare our mother had perfected.

I think that talent skipped me entirely.

"Okay," I said, stepping towards the entrance. "You're sure it's safe?" I had to close my eyes and breathe out, long and slow. It was okay, it would all be okay. My sister was here and she would look after me. It was what sisters did.

It was what Grace did. Not so much what I did, though I wanted, so badly, not to be the screw-up everyone thought I was. I could start by following through on this. If I just tried…

"Come on, I've been here before. It's a good one to start on." She grabbed my arm and squeezed it reassuringly when I reached her side. "So, in you go!" Grace grinned, her teeth white against pink lips. Why was she wearing lipstick? Why was I thinking about that?

I took one step into the mouth of that cave. It was as if the world had been left behind until Grace stepped in and nudged me with her elbow.

"Come on, slow-poke, you know Mum hates it when we're late for dinner."

Grace moved ahead with the easy confidence of someone who'd done this time and time again, so it was a relief to be behind her, to not have her gaze on me as I found my feet and stumbled against some rocks, her shoes clunky on my feet despite us being the same size.

Grace stopped and waited for me to catch up. "You ready to go?"

I let out a breath and looked where she pointed. The path wasn't too steep, winding down in a switchback fashion, littered with rocks of every size. Grace reached over and turned on my headlamp, grinning as the light splashed against her face.

"Come on. You're going to love it when we get to the bottom. There are some amazing formations."

She rambled on as we walked. Grace could speak for hours on her passions, and more than anything I think she was just pleased to be able to share it with me, even if under duress. It wasn't that I didn't want to be there, specifically. I didn't want to be anywhere, and I didn't think any amount of beauty, or awe, would pull me from that feeling. Life was hard, my brain was my enemy, and I was too tired to fight anymore.

I almost walked straight into her back; she gave a small gasp and turned to glare at me.

I could see it there, sickly green and poisonous purple curling out of her mouth with her breath, with the word, "Watch—" She stopped. Exhaled. "Sorry, you gave me a fright, and didn't I tell you to watch out?" She gripped my arm again, harder than before. "You have to be careful. I know I said it was safe, but it's only safe if you pay attention all the time."

"Okay," I said, flinching back from the colours in the air between us. I didn't need any of that in my body; it was toxic enough as it was. "Do we have to go down?"

She nodded, then unhooked her drink bottle and took a swig. She offered it to me, but I shook my head. "We have to abseil, do you remember how I showed you?"

I nodded again, wishing I'd had that water but too frozen now to get my bottle out. We'd practiced this before, but I wasn't ready. Might not ever be ready.

"Izzy, it's going to be okay. You were great at the climbing wall, you just need to do the same here. Pretend we're back at the YMCA. You're safe. We're together. There's a permanent anchor here, and we're going to use that."

Permanent. I looked down the cliff face. It wasn't smooth, dotted with rocks of all shapes and sizes, thankfully not a straight drop.

"How do we get back up? I can't climb this." I stepped back

from the edge, panic coming over me again, red and tight and twisting.

"Izzy," Grace said sharply. She gripped my chin and made me look at her. So serene. She was always so much calmer than me, as if she'd got all those genes and I'd got … something else.

"The cave has another exit so you don't have to climb up. It's going to be okay, and I promise, everything you're feeling now? It's worth it."

"Okay."

"Trust me?"

I nodded and licked my lips, so dry they felt like they would split.

"Come on." She got me hooked up and helped me to the edge. This time it was me who grabbed her hand.

"Thank you," I said, hoping that by the meagre light of our torches she could see that I meant for more than this trip. "I owe you."

She grinned as I assumed the right pose and dropped over the edge of the ledge.

"Nice form, Izzy. You've got this!" she called down to me.

The rope was strong in my hand, the fibres digging gently into my skin, assuring me I had a good grip. I held my breath as I lowered myself, feet braced against the rocks, back leaning into the abyss. Darkness embraced me as I swung my head down so that the torch beam swept below.

"I can't see the bottom." My voice quavered.

"It's there. Trust me." Her voice was strong, steady as always. Was she ever afraid? "I've done this before, hundreds of times."

"Okay." I sent the word up like a prayer to Grace, my new goddess as I dropped into the cave. I lowered myself another few metres and looked again, but still no sign of the ground. An ache was gnawing at my chest. I was about to call up again when the rope moved in my hand. No, not the rope, the world.

Rocks clattered beside me, stumble-tripping their way to the floor.

"Grace!"

"I'm here. Just hang tight. It's a little quake." But there was a thread of fear in her voice now, it slithered down the rope and took up residence in my brain.

There was a sharp jolt and I cracked against the cliff face. My helmet protected my head, but my elbow and knees jarred against the rocks. I cried out and I knew there would be blood.

"Izzy!" Grace yelled. I looked up. Saw the light from her torch as I spun and crashed against the wall of the cliff, bright in the darkness.

"Don't fall. Help me." I didn't know if the two things could be done in tandem. Her light disappeared, but I felt a tug on the rope and I held my breath, closed my eyes. I could try to climb, but then I'd be pulling on the rope too, and that wouldn't help, would it? I didn't know. I didn't know anything. I gripped the rock face, finding crevices to dig my feet into.

The thudding of my heart was there, loud but alone. No more clatter of rocks, just my breath hitting the wall.

"I'm going to get you up." Grace's voice was comforting.

"Okay," I said.

She tugged on the rope and I shifted my foot, trying to gain some height, to help.

"Wait," she said, her voice frantic. "Don't move."

"Grace? You're freaking me out."

"I just—"

There was a rumble. The wall rippled and rolled. The sound of the rope breaking seemed loud over the roar of the earthquake and I fell and fell and fell.

* * *

I knew I wasn't dead because everything hurt. I tried to move my hand but couldn't. I realised I was stuck in mud so thick it felt like drying cement.

"Grace!" I yelled, but the only response was my voice ricocheting off the walls.

I couldn't see a thing. Were my eyes even open? Did it matter? I was stuck at the bottom of a hole with no way out. I hadn't realised until then that I actually did want to live, that despite my strange quirks and inability to hold down a job or succeed in the way normal people did, I wanted life.

A low hum filled the space. I held my breath, waiting for rocks to crash down and crush me. Tears leaked out the corners of my closed eyes; a high-pitched squeal stole out of my lungs. Something tickled along my spine and I shuddered. This was fear, I told myself, fear making me feel things that couldn't be there, but then a tendril of something seemed to curl around my ankle, to tug my foot deeper into the mud. My squeal turned into a scream, which sparked like tiny glow worms expelled into the darkness.

I struggled, fighting to free myself from the mud, but my violent attempts to move only seemed to make it clamp down on me harder.

"No! No! I don't want to die in here. I don't want to die." I sobbed, sank, my chest heavy.

If I free you, will you free me?

The voice trickled into my brain with the sensation of warm honey, of melted butter, the scent of toast in my nostrils, of comfort, of home. I relaxed. I couldn't help it, it was so soothing.

Sure, I thought to the figment of my imagination. No idea how to do that, but if it gets me out of here … Wait. What are you?

It was an invitation. Something thin and sharp pierced my neck and I screamed again, light blooming behind my eyes, and then I could see … something large as it soared through the sky, its wings – no not wings, fins? – large and wide and trailing, trailing. I couldn't fathom it. It was too big, too much. Stars burst from the night sky, swimming past me so quickly, and then I could see other great beasts, wondrous, ponderous creatures moving through space, through time and infinity. They were deep blue, sparkling, shining. I didn't know. I couldn't comprehend. It was …

When Māui caught this fish I was not in the sea but in the sky and he pinned me down beneath these rocks, grew an island on me.

It unfolded in the style of the books of legends from my youth, Māui, strong and brave, half god, half mortal, his feet planted firmly on the ground, but instead of capturing the sun he was capturing this beast, tearing it from the sky with brute force. Everything collapsed back to darkness, the weight of it crushing me the same way the weight of all these rocks weighed down the beast.

"Have you been here all this time?" I asked.

So long. But I still remember.

Another flash of the stars and some ineffable, indescribable sensation that pressed my brain so hard I almost passed out. And grief. It crushed me, made me want to curl into a little ball, and then my arms were loose, my legs too, and I was folded in on myself. The images in my head of the things that were lost overwhelmed me, threatening to tip me into oblivion.

The creature pulled back, but I held my ball tight, eyes pressed shut, still seeing stars.

"Make it stop!"

Make me free.

I'd have gone crazy – hell, I was halfway there and I'd not suffered anything like this creature had: suffering inflicted by one of my kind. That thought sped through my brain, bouncing off the pieces of me that I kept locked in boxes, stirring up anxiety.

"Anything, just make it stop. Make it stop and promise that my sister will be safe."

Everything went still, the silence so quiet that it buzzed in my ears. I dropped my hands from my head, uncurled my limbs and sat.

"I don't know how to save you," I whispered. "I don't—"

As I have been your vessel for all these years, so too shall you be mine.

Pain fired through my synapses, burning me out until everything went black.

GRACE

I paced outside the perimeter the rescue team had set up. They'd been here for hours and Izzy was somewhere down there, underneath it all. I couldn't breathe. It was my job to keep her safe and she might be dead, right now, trapped under layers of rock, her body twisted and broken the same way her mind seemed to be sometimes.

Mum was going to kill me. She'd already called, her voice so frantic I couldn't understand what she was saying. A doctor had to tranquilise her and she was at home with Dad while I paced, wearing a trench in the ground, cursing it for the terrible quake that had probably murdered my sister.

"Grace?"

I turned. It was Izzy. I inhaled, relief filling me. She was alive, she was okay, and she was crawling from the rubble in a completely different spot to where the rescue team were searching. I ducked under the perimeter tape and scrambled to her.

"You're alive," I whispered, holding her at arm's length. I didn't want to draw attention, to call for help. I needed to make sure she was okay first. She let me wipe the blood from her neck with my fingers, let me check for breaks, before I crushed her into a hug. "I can't believe it. I thought … I thought I'd lost you. I—"

"It's okay," she said. She smiled, a beatific glint in her eyes. "I'm okay. Actually, I'm better than ever."

I frowned. It wasn't the response I expected, given her predilection for anxiety. No, that was too harsh of me. It wasn't her fault that her nerves seemed to eat her alive. She was sensitive to the world around her, open and aware in a way that others didn't seem to be, and I loved that about her, even if it meant she needed my help. Even if it meant I couldn't go and live the life I'd always wanted to. She was more important.

Izzy's inability to function as a normal person had often driven Mum and Dad to distraction. I felt that if she'd had an official diagnosis of some kind it would have made it easier on all of us. I liked to think of her as a modern shaman, but then maybe that was just a coping mechanism. She was a dreamy woman, and with a little focus could make some good money from her art; it just never seemed to happen.

"Over here!" I heard a shout, and then I was pulled away from Izzy as a medical team looked her over.

She had mild concussion and was free of major injury, just cuts on her limbs, her cheek, and her neck. She'd been very lucky, but the way she looked at me now ... I couldn't help but wonder. Just what had happened down there to cause this shift in her behaviour?

* * *

It started off as just notes for the doctor. He wanted me to keep tabs on Izzy, make sure there were no lingering effects from the concussion, to keep track of her behaviour in case she needed counselling from the trauma she'd been through.

There was some dizziness, she vomited once, and her expression was vague when I asked her about specific things. Other than that she seemed fine – more than fine, she seemed better than ever. She had gained focus, was doing some kind of research online, tinkering with some ... device. I didn't know what it was and she wasn't saying a peep. She would just grin at me, with that strange gleam in her eyes, and tell me that I'd find out soon enough.

Some nights I would find her sitting on the balcony, her legs swinging over the edge and her gaze fixated on the night sky, a deep sense of yearning etching her face.

"Haven't you ever wanted to escape, to fly away?"

I bit my tongue, held back the words that would hurt her. But then she looked at me and I had to be honest. "You know I have."

"I do. That was a test." She smiled, but then she worried her bottom lip between her teeth. "I'm sorry. I know it's my fault."

"No, don't ever say that. I chose this. I chose you. You're my sister and I love you so much." I slipped my hand into hers and she squeezed it, her skin feeling drier than it normally did. "I might have wanted other things – I might still get other things – but this is what I want right now."

"I'm going to give you the universe," she whispered, eyes filled with adoration.

There was something about the way she said it that sent a shiver down my spine. As if she really meant it, in a way I couldn't comprehend.

"Come on, come inside and I'll make us some hot chocolate before bed."

"No," she said softly, letting our hands drift apart. "I want to stay out here for a bit. I'll see you in the morning." She smiled again, but I knew I was dismissed.

* * *

A week later she was out of the apartment on some furtive mission. This whole secrecy thing she had going on was driving me mad and her door was slightly ajar, so I pushed it open a little wider and peered inside.

Her room was chaos. That … machine, no, machines … took prime place on her desk and there were scattered drawings around it. I stepped inside and felt anxious as I tiptoed across to her desk. Some of the drawings were of the machines, or what I assumed were parts, maybe, for inside it. Schematics? None of it made sense to me. There were maps of the area where we'd gone

caving, scrawled with distances and depths. Others were drawings of space, some familiar celestial bodies and others I couldn't
identify. The artwork evoked a sense of longing, through some
ineffable quality. It made my stomach ache, made me need to
get out, get away from there, pretend I'd seen nothing. I turned
towards the door and my mouth dropped open. I tried to take in
the image on the wall. It was…

It was stars and dark skies. It was some creature I couldn't
understand, sprawling across the wallpaper, trailing dust and debris behind it, leaving fire in its wake. It was dark and vibrant
and vivid and more than alive. I fell to my knees, all the strength
leaving me at the sight of this great beast. What was this? What
was going through Izzy's mind?

I turned to see Izzy standing in the doorway. I looked at her
and felt guilt and shame. I reached out my hand, my head shaking, trying to find the words to apologise for my intrusion.

"It's beautiful, isn't it?" She smiled. "You like it don't you?"
Her eyes were fixed on the wall, but all I could see was her.

Something was wrong. Something more than strange drawings and stranger machinery. She wasn't acting like Izzy, who
would normally have screamed at me to get out, to respect her
privacy, who could have ignored me for days in a cold fury or
sobbed for a week at my invasion.

"I've never seen anything like it," I said, the only words I
could think of that were honest. "Where … Where did you see
this?"

She turned to face me, that glint returning to her eyes. "Under
the ground. I saw a lot of things under the ground."

"Izzy, I'm worried about you." I bit my lip. "I think we should
go and see someone. That you should … I don't know, get some

counselling for the trauma? You were trapped underground for hours, it's only sense that—"

"Okay," she said, and then she added, "but first I want to show you something. Why don't you make an appointment for two days' time, and tomorrow, I'll show you?"

Did I dare ask what? And why wasn't she fighting me? "Okay," I said, the words dull in my mouth. I didn't know how to respond to this person. I didn't know how I felt anymore.

Izzy came and gave me a hug, then ushered me from the room. "I just have to finish this little project before we can go tomorrow. I'll see you in the morning." She gently pushed me into the hallway and I heard the lock click into place.

* * *

I was drinking coffee, waiting for Izzy to emerge from her room when the front door opened. She was a mess, mud flecking her jeans from hem to knee. Dirt caked her fingers and streaked her face.

"Where the hell have you been?" I asked, rushing to her side. "Are you okay?"

She grinned. "I'm fine. Totally fine, in fact I'm amazing. Are you ready?"

I frowned. "What, now? Don't you need to get cleaned up? Where have you been?"

"I'll show you. I promise, you just have to come. Get some sensible shoes on, and say goodbye to the real world for now."

"The real—" I shook my head. "Fine, whatever. I'll get my shoes." She was back to being dreamy, to making no sense, and in a way that was comforting. I headed down the hallway to my room to find my sneakers, pulling them on and grabbing a jacket. As I walked back to the lounge I stopped outside Izzy's room. Her desk was clear. The devices gone. I opened my mouth, but Izzy called.

"Hurry up! We need to go." That impatience was all her. I shook off the worry and followed her out the door, and downstairs to the car.

Izzy slipped into the driver's seat, taking control with an ease I'd never seen in her. She hummed an upbeat tune, and seemed not to hear my constant questions as to where we were going and why. I gave up, leaned into the headrest and closed my eyes. I'd just have to wait.

When we drew to a stop I opened my eyes and let out a gasp. The caves. We were at the caves.

"Why? Why here?" My heart thudded and my ears buzzed. It was too soon, barely a week since the earthquake. We were still having aftershocks! Barely a week since I thought I'd lost her forever.

"Because I made a promise down there, deep in the ground, and I need to follow though. I need to show you."

Izzy got out of the car and waited for me to do the same. My knees felt wobbly, but she seemed sure and confident, and I didn't know what magic it was that had changed our roles. Was this how she normally felt: cautious and scared and uncertain of her place in the world?

The buzzing in my ears only intensified. I stopped walking, but she grabbed my hand and pulled me, stronger than I had ever imagined her to be. We reached the place where she'd emerged what seemed a lifetime ago, reborn into this other person who held my hand.

"Come on. We have to crawl." She let go and disappeared between two rocks, contorting her body.

"I don't want to go," I said, my voice a whisper. How could she be this brave?

"You have to." Her voice was tense, but then she sighed, relaxed her shoulders. "Remember how you made me? You knew it would be good for me, and it was. Now it's your turn to trust me. I need to give you something."

There was nothing I wanted in that hole in the ground, but I forced myself to inch forward, to twist my body, to fit myself between those rocks despite the fact it made me shudder, made bile burn at the back of my throat.

When I was through the gap the tunnel widened slightly, its walls were eerily smooth in the faint light from outside, too round and perfect to be natural. My thoughts skittered away from what that might mean.

Izzy passed me a headlamp and I pulled it on, comforted by the familiar movement. I turned the light on and the beam exposed the tunnel – it was steep, but not too steep, and Izzy was already heading down.

"You've been here before, haven't you?" I asked. My voice bounced weirdly off the walls as though the acoustics didn't quite match up to the dimensions.

"Yeah. There's just something about it."

I could hear that damned smile in her voice. I just wanted it to stop. A pang of guilt hit me; I didn't want her to be miserable, but this … joy, this inner happiness wasn't real, it wasn't her.

"How long until we get there?" The wash of emotions, the confines of the space – this place – were all crushing in on me and I needed out. But not without her.

"Soon. I promise. You're doing great."

"That's something I normally say to you." My knees hurt. My hands. My heart. I could only focus on the movement, nothing beyond my body, beyond the figure in front of me.

"I learned from the best." Izzy laughed. "Come on, just a little further."

Then there was a rush of cooler air. It wasn't fresh but it signalled open space and I pushed on, past my fear and into the open cavern. I cast my light around, trying to see why it was she'd brought me here. She took my light off me and turned on a lantern.

It was just a cave. One of her devices was propped against one of the far walls, but otherwise there was nothing here. I was disappointed. Comforted.

"Is this where you landed?" I asked.

"Almost." Izzy grabbed my hand and pulled me forward. She pointed at a shape on the ground. "There. That's the outline of me. It was mud when I landed. It's gotten harder since then."

"Is this what you needed me to see?" I frowned, not sure what purpose it served.

"Not quite."

She pulled me into a hug, held me close. I stroked her hair, inhaled the smell of her, not quite pleasant but infinitely Izzy. When she pulled away there were tears in her eyes. She pointed at the spot on the ground again. "Lie down and look up."

"Why are you crying?" I asked, rubbing my thumbs across her cheeks, wiping the tears away.

"Because I love you so much. You have no idea."

"I think I do, kiddo. Kind of love you too." I smiled at her, relaxing now. Everything was going to be okay.

I sat down in the space she'd pointed and then lay in the groove her body had left. It seemed to tighten around me, softer than I expected, warmer too. I looked up at the ceiling of the cave. Izzy switched off the lantern and I could see...

Stars. I could see the vastness of space. She'd painted it there in phosphorescence, just like the one on her wall. How had she got so high?

I tried to sit up but the ground held me tight. Something tickled the back of my neck and then pain burst through me, something else, too.

"Izzy, what did you do?" I cried.

"I wanted to give you the galaxy, Grace. You'll see things you never could have imagined. He said he would keep you safe." Izzy leaned down and kissed my forehead. "Don't struggle. It'll just make it worse." She was crying harder now as she pulled a remote from her pocket, and I couldn't move my head enough to track her movement, but she was going away, leaving me here, trapped in the ground.

"Who is he?" I yelled after her.

I am Te Ika.

I heard a beep, and then the earth rumbled, shifted, tugged at what held me. More noises, followed by another and another. Explosions. The ground shivered and shook and rocks crashed from the ceiling. I struggled, trying to cover my head, to curl into a ball, but something kept the debris from hitting me. There was a ripple, a huge shudder and then I was moving, lifting, sliding through rock, plumes of dust, walls of noise, and then clearing the ground and breaching the clouds.

The world fell away as the creature slowly absorbed me, absorbed my fears about what was happening to the island below.

The hum of Izzy's tune was the only thing I could hear…
And then there were only stars.

GIRLS WHO DO NOT DROWN
ANDI C. BUCHANAN

There are girls who stumble along the beach, barefoot, heels in one hand and a premixed drink in the other, balancing upon the line between the smothering land and the vicious sea, hoping they won't see morning.

There are girls who will, in the last moments of their lives, fingers clutching the soaking mane of the beast below them out of pure instinct, blame themselves for seeking adventure, for finding exhilaration in danger. There are girls who know that if they make it home, they will be blamed or mocked because who could be interested enough in ugly girls like them to tempt them below the waves?

There are girls who do not know they are girls until the sea comes for them.

There are girls who have been told the old stories, who know the old ways to resist, to save themselves. And there are girls who find their own ways.

* * *

There is Alice on an angry winter night, on a beach full of scattered cigarettes and the smell of spilled rum and vomit on the rocks. There are waves crashing in, dirty white foam just visible in the moonlight. The remnants of the bonfire glow and fade behind her. Her friends have gone home, or have wandered back into the town and passed out on the sofas of friends with more liberal or more absent parents, and now there is just Alice on the beach. No-one calls her Alice, not yet and perhaps not ever, and she wonders, as many girls do when they're fifteen, whether anyone will even notice if she disappears.

She's been at a beach party, which happens any time the rain is light enough to get a fire going and the cold is just bearable. They stoke the flames and share drinks and smokes and dare each other to make a move on one of the older girls, the ones with hair tugged back until it hurts and gold-hoop earrings. Alice has poured some of the rum she shoplifted from the co-op into her water bottle and added a can of Sprite, and she has a new packet of ciggies. If it wasn't for everything else, life would be good.

Alice doesn't want to go home, so she climbs over the rocks and finds a space to watch the waves in the dark. And just like in the stories, a glashtyn approaches her.

* * *

This is an island that sends all its girls into the sea. The lucky ones will float, encased in steel or wood. They'll come back with teaching diplomas, or they'll come back by noon, following boats laden with herring, and they'll work until dusk, until the catch is gutted and salted and barrelled, until their fingers are chafed raw with salt. The others will not come back, or decades will be lost and themselves Changed when they return.

This island sends its girls into the sea, into the untamed grey sea of December, the sharp blue sea of June. It sends them from its hidden beaches and from its rebuilt ports. It sends them alone, bare feet on the stone steps cut into the cliff, and it sends them with their friends, on days that smell of salt and sunshine and wide-open futures.

The sea claims its girls, and they will say, in the Methodist church and in the Rotary meetings, that it's so very sad they were pulled to the sea, and no-one will ever stop to consider that it was they who sent their girls there. The girls who don't come back will be forgotten, and those who return will have children and rent flats in old, converted hotels and never speak of how much they fear for their daughters.

If you were to question why so many girls are lost, they would tell you that if you don't like how things are, you don't have to stay here; that there's always a boat in the morning. The sea is always waiting.

* * *

The glashtyn is tall, with dark curls and eyes that glint even in the darkness. Pointed ears poke through his hair: donkey ears, glashtyn ears.

"I can see your ears right there." Alice holds her cigarette in her mouth and forms triangles with her fingers on each side of her head. "You're not kidding anyone."

The glashtyn smiles, huge, blunt teeth too big for his jaw, and holds out a string of pearls.

"Oh," Alice chortles mockingly. "Are these for my grandma?"

The glashtyn says nothing. His smile becomes deeper. Alice finishes her cigarette and takes a gulp from her "water" bottle, then another.

"Look, I know what I have to do. I'm not thick. I just have to wait this out till morning. Sure, I can do that. I'll get grounded, but I'm always fucking grounded. I don't really care. And no offence there, but you're hardly a temptation."

The glashtyn takes no offence. He motions for her to take the pearls. Alice shakes her head. If anyone else were here, they would find the scene absurd; Alice still looks every bit the boy she isn't, with her close-cropped hair and buttoned shirt, her baggy jeans. Everyone knows that glashtyn only appear to girls.

When he tries moving closer towards her, Alice makes the ears again, giggles, drops her bottle into a rock pool, and half-falls in her attempt to retrieve it.

"You're hardly my biggest problem anyway," she continues, her drunkenness dulling the pain of her twisted ankle. "If you can tell … if you can see what I'm hiding, it's only a matter of time before someone else does as well. And I can't … I can't stay here if that happens."

She may as well be talking to the tide, to the cold air, to the edge of a storm on the horizon, but the glashtyn is still there and he walks forward a step and holds out the pearls as if offering a solution.

"We're both pretending to be something we're not. We both know each other's secret. You're a cabbyl ushtey, a water horse, and I'm a girl. Both masquerading as men, or in my case, just a boy, as my mother likes to remind me. So, how about we both agree that there's no point us sitting here staring at each other, that you're not going to trick me, you're not going to drag me into the sea, down to my death."

But the glashtyn says nothing, and Alice waits on the rock

and wishes he'd stop grinning at her, drinking until the night sky spins high above her, wishing she was anywhere but here.

* * *

It's not that the people here don't love their daughters. They love them fiercely, squalling babies that command so much love it hurts, smart young women who play the flute and babysit their siblings and make their grandparents smile with pride. The sea cannot take the girls when they are young and their parents watch as they engage this force with fearlessness, skipping over its waves, damming the streams that trickle from springs down the beach with rocks and wet sand. When these girls get older, their parents, knowing the sea will take them, can only hope that the sea will also bring them home.

It's not that they don't love their daughters. It's just that this is how it's always been, and that history is stronger than love, and that the sea is stronger than them all.

* * *

Alice steadies herself to the roar of the sea, seeming to come from all around her. She's nauseous and her head is beginning to thump, and the sea is drawing her to it.

Alice would never have mistaken the glashtyn for a human, would never be tempted by jewellery or romance, she's too smart for that, but she's tempted by the sea. She's tempted by escape.

The glashtyn disappears with the dawn, fading into the low cloud, or perhaps running to the sea so fast that Alice doesn't see him go. She's lasted the night; she's saved herself.

She smokes a cigarette, stubs out the end on a rock. She strips down to her boxers.

She walks into the sea.

* * *

There are girls who walk into the sea because their mothers once walked into the sea, and there are girls who walk into the sea because their mothers told them not to.

There are girls for whom the sea bends, refreshing on a warm day, to carry them wherever they might want to go. There are girls who know right from the start that they will drown.

There are girls who have been training in the council pool three times a week since they were five, and yet their limbs freeze when the first wave hits. There are girls who have always avoided the water, who find swimming comes by instinct.

There are girls who do not drown.

* * *

Alice has to get away from here. She has to get away before someone finds out what she is. She knows what happens to girls like her; knows that when girls like her are sent to the sea, they are already bloody and bruised; knows that girls like her are always meant to drown. The water reaches her stomach, an icy shock always, but she forces herself to keep going, launches herself into swimming, throws herself upon the waves. She takes long strokes, one after another, pulling herself into the cold water as the village wakes behind her.

Alice is a strong swimmer, but she knows she has no hope of

getting to the mainland. The only thing she can do is give her mother the comfort of thinking this was merely a tragic accident. She takes firm strokes, one after the other, the cold water numbing her right through, the lighthouse and the café and the lights of the small town fading behind her.

Alice is succeeding where the glashtyn has failed. Alice is drowning.

* * *

Some of the girls who do not drown spend their evenings deep in study, playing film soundtracks in their pokey bedrooms as they revise physics, history, algebra. The sea will take them on passenger ferries, and they will reserve seats with scarves and coats and head up to the deck and watch the rocky island growing smaller and smaller behind them. They will get their nursing degrees and their teaching diplomas, and they will take the ferry back for the last time, and they will walk down from the ferry, their skin dry and their hair heavy with salt, and they will feel their feet on solid ground as if for the first time.

Some of the girls who do not drown will find the herring industry in decline, barrels replaced by refrigeration, no money in following the boats. They will ask why they must go to the sea when they can become accountants and financial advisors; when they can cut hair or sell shoes or make coffee. Some of them will escape the sea. Some of them will leave and never return.

And some of the girls who do not drown will learn how to ride.

* * *

Alice swims until her arms tire and her feet feel numb with the cold and the island has faded to a rocky shadow in the distance. She feels, first, a new current beneath her and thinks nothing of it, and then hair brushes against her drooping toes and she's shocked into energy, adrenaline coursing through her. The glashtyn she outlasted has come to take her after all. It's in horse form now, but Alice knows instinctively that it's the same one; it rides alongside her, charges past her and then deep underwater before crashing upwards into her, knocking her backwards until she falls onto its back, not stopping for her to right herself, but charging on, galloping through the sea.

She clutches the sodden mane with her hands, feels the horse's heartbeat heavy between her thighs. She does not think of what's behind her and she does not think of what's beneath her; she thinks only of clinging to this beast because she knows there is nothing else to cling to.

She knows that glashtyn take girls into the sea to drown.

She knows only that she's not meant for the fate this small town has in store for her, that any choice she makes is better than choosing nothing but how things are.

Alice crashes through the surface of the water, the force of the sea smashing against her face, salt water stinging her eyes. She gasps, blinking until she can see the sun, the horizon glowing ahead, and she doesn't have time to decide if it's beautiful or menacing before she's plunged down again, clinging tightly, eyes clenched shut, her skin blue with the cold.

It might not be that she is stronger than the girls who have been taken and have drowned. It might be chance. It might be that the glashtyn has taken pity on her, though that is not something Alice has ever heard of before. It might be because she was tempted not by the glashtyn, but by the sea. She doesn't know. She only does what she has always done; she takes what she has been given and does her best to survive with it.

She rides the glashtyn through the waves, still clinging but starting to find her balance, her rhythm. She uses her whole body to guide it, pushing loudly through the waves, turning and galloping back the way they came. She begins to smile, terrified but exhilarated, breathing more easily now, holding a breath every time they plunge below the waves, relieved every time they resurface, finally accepting she's going to live.

* * *

There are girls whose need to live is stronger than their desire to die.

* * *

The whole town, and the other villages around have come out to watch, the gossip having flung itself from one stone house to another. There's a glashtyn, it said, a real glashtyn in the harbour and it looks like someone's riding it. *There's only one way one rides a glashtyn*, replied the older women, the ones who knew the old stories, *and that's down, down, down to your doom.* They barely believe, even when they see it themselves: the massive horse crashing through the water, the rider clinging desperately, but riding, not drowning.

Alice dismounts, at last, falling into shallow waters. She lingers before she leaves the sea, her mouth just above the line of the water, taking gasping, desperate breaths of air as the town blurs into view. She feels that something deep inside her is not the same, and she prays to the new god above and to Ler and his son, gods of the sea around her, that she has changed on the outside as well. She pictures herself stepping out of the water with silky black hair to her waist, delicate features, budding breasts…

She pictures a body they may drown her for, but one they will have to believe.

The cold air reveals the same scrawny, pale body she's been stuck with all her life. She doesn't let herself cry, just blinks until all the seawater from her eyes runs down her cheeks, and she sees.

The girls who swim out to bring her to shore are perhaps eight or nine years old, but they're strong and they take one arm each over their tiny shoulders and help her stand, help her walk, exhausted and breathless, one foot in front of the other, to shore. Another, even younger, splashes out to her with a towel, which she drapes around herself. These girls will not drown.

The whole town is here, but it is the girls who walk forward to her. It is the girls with plaits and the girls with fashionable bobs, girls in their hitched-up tartan skirts and girls in ragged jeans, girls who are trying not to scratch their eczema or are stumbling on twisted ankles. It is the girls with novels in their backpacks and the girls with headphones draped around their necks. It is the girls who have to leave their wheelchairs on the promenade and be helped over the sand by their friends. It is the girls who have only just realised they are girls. It is the girls who are terrified and the girls whose eyes are glistening with excitement.

Alice clutches the towel around herself and walks over the damp sand as they surround her. Some of these girls are her classmates, others she has known since they were babies. And now she smiles at her disappointment, because she knows she has not failed, that girls like her are not Changed by the fae or by the gods. Girls like her do the changing.

She will change herself, in time. Today, much more has changed. For these girls are not looking at the sea as the fate that will take them, but as a world for them to explore.

Today and tomorrow and in the warm, wild weather of spring, these girls will learn how to ride.

These girls will not drown.

ABOUT THE AUTHORS

ANDI C. BUCHANAN lives in Lower Hutt, surrounded by books and robotic insects. Their fiction is published or forthcoming in *Fireside, Apex, Kaleidotrope, Glittership*, and more, and their editing has been recognised on the Tiptree Award Honor List. You can find Andi on Twitter @andicbuchanan or at www.andicbuchanan.org.

OCTAVIA CADE is a New Zealand writer with a PhD in science communication from the University of Otago. She's had close to 50 short stories published in various markets, including *Clarkesworld, Asimov's*, and *Shimmer*. Octavia has also had several novellas and a nonfiction collection of essays on food and horror published, and she has a cli-fi novel, *The Stone Wētā*, due out in 2020 from Paper Road Press. She reviews regularly for *Strange Horizons*, has won three Sir Julius Vogel awards for speculative writing here in New Zealand, and attended the Clarion West Writing Workshop in 2016. She will be the 2020 Square Edge/ Massey University writer in residence.

MARK ENGLISH is an ex-astrophysicist who became a space scientist working on the Cassini/Huygens mission to Saturn. Computer and high energy research followed, including a stint at the JET Fusion Torus in Oxfordshire, UK. All this high falutin' science hasn't damped his love of fiction. It has, however, ruined his enjoyment of rainbows, colourful flames on romantic log fires and rings around the moon.

Mark's work has also appeared on *Everyday Fiction*, *Raygun Revival*, *Escape Pod* and *Perihelion*. He has also been published on *Antipodean SF*, where he has narrated several stories.

A.J. FITZWATER is a dragon wearing a human meat suit living between the cracks of Christchurch, New Zealand. Their short fiction has appeared in *Clarkesworld*, *Beneath Ceaseless Skies*, *Shimmer Magazine*, a variety of New Zealand and international anthologies, and other venues of repute. In 2020, their capybara pirate collection *The Voyages of Cinrak The Dapper* will be published by Queen of Swords Press and their WWII Land Girls shape-shifter novella *No Man's Land* by Paper Road Press.

MELANIE HARDING-SHAW is a speculative fiction writer, policy geek, and mother-of-three from Wellington. Her work has appeared in publications like *Breach Zine*, *Daily Science Fiction*, and *The Arcanist*. You can find her on Facebook @MelanieHardingShawWriter and Twitter @MelHardingShaw, and at www.melaniehardingshaw.com.

CASSIE HART (Ngāi Tahu) is a writer of speculative fiction and lover of pizza, coffee, and zombies (in no particular order). She's had short stories published in several anthologies, and has been a finalist for both the Sir Julius Vogel and Australian Shadow Awards, and was a mentee in the Te Papa Tupu mentorship programme in 2018.

ISABELLE MCNEUR studies at Victoria University, where she has completed several IIML courses and won the Prize for Best Original Composition in 2017. She has been published in journals such as *Starling, Aotearotica, Flash Frontier, NZ Poetry Yearbook, Wizards in Space* and *Headland*. She hopes to one day be financially stable enough to adopt a dog.

SEAN MONAGHAN writes from a quiet nook in the corner of his 100-year-old home in Palmerston North. A Sir Julius Vogel Award winner, Sean studied Creative Writing at the University of Queensland and Victoria University. His stories have appeared in *Landfall, Takahe* and *Te Kōrero Ahi Kā*, among others.

DAVE MOORE is an Auckland-based writer and graduate of the AUT Masters in Creative Writing (2016). His work has appeared in *Landfall* and the Cloud Ink *Fresh Ink* anthologies in 2017 and 2019.

JAMES ROWLAND is a New Zealand-based, British-born writer. His work has previously appeared at *Aurealis, Black Dandy* and *Compelling Science Fiction*. 'The Glassblower's Peace' was a finalist in the Sir Julius Vogel Awards 2018 for Best Novella/Novelette. When he's not moonlighting as a writer of magical, strange or futuristic stories, he works as an intellectual property lawyer. Besides writing, his hobbies are reading, stand-up comedy, travel, photography, and the sport of kings – cricket. You can find more of his work at his website www.jamesrowlandwriter. wordpress.com.

GRANT STONE's stories and poems have appeared in *Island, Strange Horizons, Shimmer, Andromeda Spaceways Inflight Magazine* and *Semaphore,* and have twice won the Sir Julius Vogel Award. Grant lives in Auckland and is a proud member of SpecFicNZ.

M. DARUSHA WEHM is the Nebula Award-nominated and Sir Julius Vogel Award-winning author of the interactive fiction game *The Martian Job,* as well as the science fiction novels *Beautiful Red, Children of Arkadia, The Voyage of the White Cloud,* and the Andersson Dexter cyberpunk detective series. Their mainstream books include the *Devi Jones' Locker* YA series and the humorous coming-of-age novel *The Home for Wayward Parrots.* Darusha's short fiction and poetry have appeared in many venues, including *Terraform* and *Nature.* Originally from Canada, Darusha now lives in Wellington, New Zealand after spending several years sailing the Pacific.

TONI WI is a speculative fiction writer from New Zealand. She likes space opera and flash fiction, and is currently working on a novel. You can find her on Twitter @toniwaiaroha.

ACKNOWLEDGEMENTS

No reprint anthology could exist without stories to reprint. Thanks and acknowledgements are due to all the editors and publishers who originally found the stories featured in this collection and first brought them to light:

Strange Horizons, which first published Octavia Cade's 'We Feed the Bears of Fire and Ice';

Clarkesworld, which first published A.J. Fitzwater's 'Logistics';

Wizards in Space, which first published Isabelle McNeur's 'The Garden';

Breach Magazine, which first published Toni Wi's 'Trees';

Terraform, which first published M. Darusha Wehm's 'A Most Elegant Solution';

Abyss & Apex, which first published Mark English's 'Mirror Mirror';

Steve Proposch, Christopher Sequeira and Bryce Stevens, who first published Grant Stone's 'A Brighter Future' and J.C. Hart's 'Te Ika', in *Cthulhu: Land of the Long White Cloud* (*IFWG Publishing Australia*);

Landfall, which first published Dave Moore's 'The People Between the Silences';

Wild Musette Journal, which first published Melanie Harding-Shaw's 'Common Denominator';

Asimov's Science Fiction, which first published Sean Monaghan's 'The Billows of Sarto';

Aurealis Magazine, which first published James Rowland's 'The Glassblower's Peace';

and *Apex*, which first published Andi C. Buchanan's 'Girls Who Do Not Drown'.

ALSO FROM PAPER ROAD PRESS

FROM A SHADOW GRAVE
ANDI C. BUCHANAN

Wellington, 1931. Seventeen-year-old Phyllis Symons's body is discovered in the Mount Victoria tunnel construction site.

Eighty years later, Aroha Brooke is determined to save her life.

"Haunting in every sense of the word"
– Charles Payseur, Quick Sip Reviews

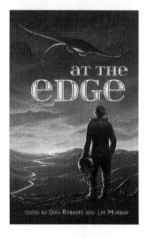

AT THE EDGE
EDITED BY DAN RABARTS AND LEE MURRAY

From the brink of civilisation, the fringe of reason, and the border of reality, come 22 stories infused with the bloody-minded spirit of the Antipodes.

Winner of the Sir Julius Vogel Award for Best Collected Work, 2017

"Lovecraftian horrors to please the most cosmic of palates" – Angela Slatter

ALSO FROM PAPER ROAD PRESS

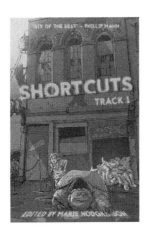

SHORTCUTS: TRACK 1
EDITED BY MARIE HODGKINSON

Strange tales of Aotearoa New Zealand. Seven Kiwi authors weave stories of people and creatures displaced in time and space, risky odysseys, and dangerous discoveries.

Winner of the Sir Julius Vogel Award for Best Novella: Octavia Cade, *The Ghost of Matter*

"Six of the best" – Phillip Mann

BABY TEETH: BITE-SIZED TALES OF TERROR
EDITED BY DAN RABARTS AND LEE MURRAY

Kids say the creepiest things. Twenty-seven stories about the strange, unexpected, and downright terrifying sides of parenthood.

Leave the lights on tonight. So you'll see them coming.

Winner of the Sir Julius Vogel Award for Best Collected Work, 2014
Winner of the Australian Shadows Award for Edited Publication, 2014

Printed in Great Britain
by Amazon

13057558R00119